ALL ABOUT EVE

Patty Copeland

ZEBRA BOOKS
KENSINGTON PUBLISHING CORP.

To Margaret Watson with thanks for the veterinary advice. And to John Lane, my dad, who first believed in my dream.

ZEBRA BOOKS are published by

Kensington Publishing Corp.
850 Third Avenue
New York, NY 10022

First Zebra Printing: June, 1996
10 9 8 7 6 5 4 3 2 1

Printed in the United States of America

Prologue

It wasn't every day you learned of your fiancé's extracurricular activities by eavesdropping in the ladies' room. Eve Sutton looked at her newly bared left hand, still trembling from the confrontation with Richard. Her *ex*-fiancé. Huddling deeper into her sable, she sank back on the rear seat of the limousine as it eased into the northbound traffic of Michigan Avenue.

How could she have made such a terrible mistake?

Eve stared through the tinted windows at couples strolling along Chicago's Magnificent Mile. When the car stopped at a red light, she glanced across lanes of traffic to the old Water Tower where little white Italian lights swayed in the wind-tossed trees of early May. Several horse and buggy rigs awaited passengers. The night was too cold for a carriage ride, but she remembered last summer when Richard had insisted a ride was just the thing to take her mind off everything. An old familiar ache rose and sharpened once again.

That had been the beginning.

She'd been stunned by her father's sudden death and unable to cope. Richard, a rising star in her father's inner circle of command, had persisted in pulling her back into the mainstream. He'd succeeded in making her laugh again. He'd become her constant escort and finally her fiancé. Eve could see now that she'd let herself drift into the commitment of a life with Richard. What would her father have thought of his fair-haired boy if he could have overheard, as she just had, about Richard's unfaithfulness? Or Richard being unable to deny it when he caught up with her at the coat-check room?

Perhaps she was the only one who didn't know of Richard's amorous activities. Studying the back of the chauffeur's white head, Eve decided to tackle the question head-on. Who better to ask than someone who'd known her all her life?

"Simms, I broke my engagement to Richard tonight." His gaze flicked to hers via the rearview mirror, but it was too far away and too dark for her to clearly read his expression. "Tell me, what did you think of him? Honestly."

Eve saw the flash of white as he smiled in the mirror. "Well now, Miss Eve, I think that's about the best news I've heard in a *long* time. Yessiree!"

"Why, don't you like Richard?"

"Well . . . there's like, then there's like, if you know what I mean, Miss Eve. Tilly and me, we never thought he was good enough for you." He shook his head, grinning at her in the mirror. "Ummm-um! Just wait till Tilly hears." Instead of cheering her, his delight deepened her gloom.

As the car rolled northward toward the affluent suburb of Lake Forest, she tried to think of the ties that bound her to Richard. There were social engagements to cancel, and what was she to do about the office situation? By the time Simms dropped her at the front door, an incipient headache had grown to a pounding drumbeat at the realization of how far Richard had insinuated himself into her life.

Eve accessed the alarm code and let herself in. When the door closed behind her, she finally felt safe. *Safe.* The word reverberated in her head, setting off a chain reaction of thought, but the pounding in her temples increased in tempo. Massaging the area with her fingertips, she made her way slowly upstairs and collapsed on her bed in the dark.

At the sound of a slight noise a short time later, she glimpsed the shadowy form of Tilly making preparations to help her to bed. "You spoil me," Eve told the older woman, pushing herself upright on the bed, "but I love you for it."

"Now we both know, child, that I enjoy doing it, so you just relax and let me get on with it." Tilly laid a nightgown across the end of the bed, and helped her out of her coat and dress. "Simms already told me about your engagement, so don't worry yourself about how to break the news."

Eve finished undressing and, inexplicably, her eyes teared. Blinking rapidly, she pulled on her nightgown, determined not to cry. She never cried. And she knew she wasn't heartbroken, just angry. Damned angry at being used. Again.

She began to relax as Tilly repeated the ritual of her childhood for the blinding headaches brought on by stress. Humming a spiritual in time to massage strokes, her housekeeper worked her usual magic on the migraine.

Eve rolled over and caught her hand as she started to move away. "Thank you, Tilly. Most of all, thanks for being here. You and Simms both."

"Now where else would we be?" She settled back down on the edge of the bed and embraced Eve, rubbing her back with a comforting hand. "Don't fret yourself, child. And don't waste no time crying over that man," she added sternly. "He wasn't the right one for you."

Despite her efforts, tears leaked from beneath Eve's closed eyelids. "What's wrong with me, Tilly, that someone can't love me for myself? Why does it always have to be my money?"

Tilly gathered her close. "Somewhere, sometime, probably when you least expect it, sugar, some man with a clean heart and clear eyes is going to recognize what a special person you are. And it won't matter to him if you don't have a dime." She patted Eve's heaving shoulders, letting her cry it out. "Until then, child, all you can do is be yourself."

One

Eve inhaled the acrid scent of freshly turned soil from the surrounding farms as she drove through the southern Wisconsin countryside. Her car topped the hill and another valley unfolded before her. Twilight hastened to full dusk and obscured what must have been a beautiful sight as spring reclaimed the land.

She had shunned the fleet but flat expressway north for an older, undulating, four-lane highway that would take her up the middle of Wisconsin. It would take her another hour to reach the family cabin on a hidden lake, but time didn't matter any more.

Eve smiled in the darkness remembering Tilly's stunned expression when she had thanked her this morning for the idea of the great escape. Of course, she had put her own spin on Tilly's words. She was going one better than just being herself; she was going to be Evelyn Sutton, a woman without benefit of the wealth and power that usually went with her family name.

The car coughed and her smile faded. "Come on, baby," she said, patting the dashboard. "Don't let me down!"

Scanning the control panel, Eve couldn't see any warning lights on and, as nothing else happened, she gradually relaxed. She wondered what Uncle Robb would make of her choice of a used car. She wasn't too fond of the bumper stickers herself, but figured she could get rid of them with some elbow grease. All that mattered was she was happy with her decision. And that she had done it herself, all part of her do-it-yourself plan.

Again her car coughed and jerked, gave several hiccups and died. Eve steered the car to the shoulder of the road. Turning off the headlights, she waited an interminable minute and turned the key. The engine ground for a moment, but didn't catch. She counted to one hundred and tried again. Nothing.

The surrounding darkness was unbroken. She remembered passing a sign, so there must be an exit ahead off the old divided highway. Pinpricks of light appeared in the rearview mirror, growing steadily brighter while she prayed a nice little old lady would be at the wheel of the oncoming vehicle. It whizzed by. Obviously she was going to have to get out and at least stand by the car to attract attention.

In the next five minutes, the only lights she saw were those going in the opposite direction, her only company a lone cricket serenade and goosebumps. She walked briskly up and down the side of the road in front of her car, rubbing her arms when the damp chill of the spring evening seeped through her thin suede jacket.

Just when she thought she might be better off walking toward the exit somewhere ahead, she spotted a flash of light on a distant hill. Eve waited for the car to reappear on another crest, wishing she at least had a flashlight with which to signal. The headlights slowly grew in brightness. By this time she didn't care if her rescuer was male or female, just as long as someone stopped.

The headlights of the oncoming car blinded Eve as she stepped to the edge of the highway, jumping and waving her arms. A squeal of brakes rewarded her efforts to attract the driver's attention.

As it passed her, slowing to a stop, she realized the vehicle was really some sort of pickup truck. The driver threw it into reverse and backed up, pulling behind her car. She was pinned in the glow from the truck's headlights as the driver opened the door and climbed out. The first thing Eve saw in the backwash of light was the silhouette of a boot, followed by a massive body topped with a Stetson. She couldn't make out any details of the man walking toward her, back lit as he was by his own headlights; just that he was big. Very big.

" 'Evening." She jumped at the sound of his deep voice, and the man stopped beside her front car door. "Having some trouble?"

He waited patiently, his hands resting on his blue jeans-covered hips. Eve wet her lips and decided his keeping his distance was a good sign. Just to be on the safe side though, she edged toward the shoulder of the road and the opposite side of the car from him. She realized a bonus immediately as his features became clearer. He might be big, but at least he didn't look intimidating from what she could see of the illuminated half of his face. She couldn't read his expression since his mouth remained hidden under the shadow of his mustache. Wondering what the rest of his mouth looked like, she stopped herself; she'd sworn off men.

Adam Wagner's lips twitched as he watched the woman sidle around the front of the car. Hell, he supposed he couldn't blame her. She looked to be half his size and scared as a rabbit. Just what he needed at the end of a long day. He sighed. At least this woman seemed to really require some help.

At the reminder of his wasted time at Hartwig Farms because of a spoiled little rich girl, Adam grew restive with her silence. "Do you know what's wrong with the car?"

Again the woman jumped at the sound of his voice. Losing patience, he swore under his breath and braced his hands on top of the sedan. "Look, lady. You can relax. The only danger you're in is from my temper because I'm tired and hungry."

Something got through to her because her shoulders relaxed, and her face became almost pretty as it gained animation. "Really? Do you know, I think I'm hungry, too."

The woman started back toward the front of the car again and all he could see in the glare of his headlights was the washed-out features of a young woman and the blonde halo of her hair. Adam didn't know what he expected after catching a few of the slogans on the car's bumper stickers, but it certainly wasn't the low, cultured voice that had finally answered him.

"I don't know what's wrong with the car," she continued, coming to a halt in front of him. "It just stopped."

Adam frowned down at her. "Why should you take the word of a complete stranger that I mean you no harm?" When she just raised her brows, he lowered his. "I know I reassured you myself, but aren't you being just a little too trusting?"

"I admit it seems inexplicable, but somehow I just know." She shrugged and her face underwent another lightning change as she smiled. "Besides, if you'll introduce yourself, you won't be a stranger any longer."

Adam found himself intrigued, even as his temper strained against her naivete. She used words like *inexplicable* and had bumper stickers that proclaimed *Bankers Do It With Interest* and *Blondes Do It Better!* He reminded himself that he'd already been made a fool of once today and used his temper to curb his interest in this paradox who insisted on acting like a lunatic.

"And why in heaven's name were you practically dancing on the highway instead of using your emergency lights?"

"What emergency lights?"

Adam jerked open the car door and, leaning in, hit the switch that started the blinking hazard lights.

Her softly breathed "Oh" of surprise explained many things. Adam lowered himself behind the wheel of her car with difficulty and, silently mouthing an expletive, released the catch that allowed him to push the seat back. He tried the ignition, but nothing happened. He thought longingly of his dinner and wondered how long he was going to be tied up playing good Samaritan.

"If you could give me a ride to the next exit, I'm sure I can find a garage that will send someone out to pick up the car."

Adam looked at the young woman peering at him over the open car door, her bare left hand resting on the rolled-up window. "Look, Miss—" He broke off in irritation. "What's your name anyway?"

She looked self-conscious a moment, but replied, "Evelyn Sutton."

"Well, Miss Sutton, I'm afraid your confidence is misplaced. At this time on a Saturday night, you won't even find a service station open in Brighton." He slid from behind the wheel and shut the car door.

"What about farther on, maybe at the next exit?"

"Possible, but not very probable." Adam pushed the flaps of his denim jacket aside and rested his hands on his hips, grinning down at her. "I take it you're a city girl, Miss Sutton, but you're in the middle of farm country now. Things close down early around here. Besides, even if we succeeded in raising somebody on my car phone, we'd have to sit and wait more than half an hour for them to reach us. And, as my granddad used to say, my backbone is sticking to my ribs enough already."

"I assure you, Mr.—I'm sorry, you never told me your name."

"Adam Wagner. *Dr.* Adam Wagner."

"I assure you, Dr. Wagner, that if we can . . . raise someone on your car phone, I'm perfectly capable of waiting here on my own. You can continue on your way and have your dinner all that much sooner."

Before she even finished, Adam was shaking his head. "There's no way I'm going to go off and leave you out here on your own to wait for a tow truck. That's assuming we could find one." He turned away and headed for the back of his converted pickup.

"I appreciate your concern, Dr. Wagner, but—"

He stopped so suddenly that Eve ran into him full tilt trying to catch up to his giant stride. His long, muscular length was so hard, it was like running into the side of his truck. In contrast, his hands were gentle as they grasped her arms to keep her upright after bouncing off him, although his expression, what she could see of it, remained fierce.

"I'll be damned if I'm going to lie awake tonight wondering if you're safe!"

Eve looked at him in consternation. "You're to be commended for your sentiment. But I wonder, Dr. Wagner, don't your patients ever complain about your bedside manner?"

His scowl slowly changed to a grin. "Not so you'd notice."

"They're probably scared to death of you."

His grin grew. "It's all in how you handle them."

Eve knew *she* was being handled, but she glanced back toward her used car and sighed. She definitely had to get rid of those bumper stickers at the first opportunity. "I know it doesn't look like much, but it's mine. I hate to leave it to be stripped."

"What, in the middle of the country? Not likely, but we're not going to leave it." He started toward the rear of his truck again. "Besides doctoring, I also own a good-size farm. That means we have to be prepared for just about anything, including towing broken-down machinery from the fields for repair." He let down the tailgate, then found and switched on a flashlight.

As Eve moved up beside him, he flashed the light downward and warned, "Watch it or you'll bang your shin on that tow hitch." He removed a clanging piece of metal secured to the side of the truck, then handed her the flashlight. "You can hold the light for me while I attach this to your front bumper."

Less than ten minutes later, Dr. Wagner tossed his hat on the seat between them and eased the truck back onto the highway. They were on their way. Where? Eve wondered and was about to ask him when he picked up the receiver and punched a button on his cellular phone.

"Sudie, thought I'd let you know I'm running a little late. Stopped to help someone with car trouble. We're going to drop her car off at Schneider's, then come on home for dinner. And by the way, she'll be staying the night."

"Dr. Wagner—"

His gaze flicked to Eve momentarily, but he ignored her interruption and continued his conversation. "Yeah, a young lady, so I guess you'd better." He laughed at something the other person said and added, "See you in about twenty minutes."

"I appreciate your kindness," Eve said as he broke the connection, "but if you'll just drop me at the nearest motel, I can spend the night there."

"If I was to do that, Miss Sutton, I wouldn't get home to my dinner for almost another hour. As I said earlier, we're in the middle of—"

"I know, farm country." Eve sighed. "I don't mean to sound ungrateful. I've inconvenienced you and I'm sorry." She glanced across at what she could see of Dr. Wagner illuminated by the headlights' reflection. For someone so worried about his stomach, he seemed in a remarkably good mood. "It was kind of your wife to agree to my spending the night."

"I'm not married."

"Not—Then who were you talking to?"

"Sudie's my housekeeper."

"Oh." Relief that someone else would be present made Eve wilt against the cushion at her back, blushing at the interpretation she'd put on Dr. Wagner's good mood. He didn't look like a Bluebeard, but she reminded herself she'd been wrong about Richard, too. Something made her clarify Sudie's status. "I take it she lives in the house with you."

"Nope."

Eve shot forward, ramrod straight, knocking his Stetson to the floor. She stared at her supposed rescuer. "Now just a minute—" The huge grin stretched beneath his mustache alerted Eve to the fact he was having a lot of fun at her expense, and she racked her brain to recall his part of the phone conversation. Forcing herself to fold her arms and appear calm, she said as sweetly as possible, "Why don't you just explain what the sleeping arrangements are, Dr. Wagner?"

He chuckled. "For a city girl, you catch on fast." He took his eyes off the road to glance at her and, still smiling, said, "I probably should apologize for scaring the pants off you, but the chance to teach you a lesson for being so damned trusting was too good to pass up." He hit the turn signal and slowed the truck.

Eve maintained a frigid silence as they coasted to a stop. When he had again snapped on the turn signal and checked for traffic, he looked at her fully before pulling across the intersection. "Okay, I do apologize." He shrugged his massive shoulders. "Besides, if I'm honest, I was probably getting even for something that happened earlier, which had absolutely nothing to do with you."

Eve looked out the window and, unbending a little, admitted, "You're right though, Dr. Wagner. I *am* too trusting. But," she added with a determined edge, "it's something I'm working on." When she turned back, it was to intercept a piercing glance, and slowly they shared a small smile of apology.

"If you're going to be a guest, you better get used to calling me Adam."

Thinking about his smile, she barely heard his name. "Only if you call me Eve."

"Okay, Eve. To set your mind at rest, Sudie offered to spend the night when she realized I was bringing a young lady home. Since she's old enough to be my mother, she pays more attention to the conventions than I do. I have to tell you though that her offer had more to do with protecting *my* reputation than yours."

At his amused tone, Eve turned her head to see another grin spread beneath his mustache. "Ah, yes. The good doctor. Well," she murmured wickedly, "I should be able to reassure her on *that* score at least."

It was almost comical to see his mustache droop, but before she could comment on it, the truck slowed and turned into the parking lot of a dimly lit service station. Swinging wide, Adam angled her car and backed it into position beside others. Flashlight in hand, Eve swung down out of the truck to help unhitch her car.

Within a few minutes, Adam tossed the towing plate into the truck and told her to get her luggage while he rummaged for some paper to write a note. "Just set the cases by the tailgate. I'll put them in the back of the truck after I leave the note."

Her one suitcase was fairly light since she'd planned to simply rough it at the cabin, and Eve decided to heft it into the back of the truck herself as another part of her do-it-yourself improvement program. She swung the case up in an arc and stepped between the vehicles to lower it on the other side of the tailgate. And promptly rammed her left leg into the tow hitch on the back of the truck.

Her suitcase dropped with a clatter into the back of the truck, covering her exclamation of pain as she crumpled to the ground and held onto her leg where it had connected with the protruding metal triangle. She squeezed her eyes shut, moaning softly at the pain radiating up and down her leg. She didn't hear Adam's approach, but felt his hand on her shoulder as he hunched down beside her.

"Where's the flashlight?" His voice sounded calm and gentle.

"I don't know. I dropped it when I . . . hit my leg."

"Okay, sit tight. We'll soon have you fixed up."

At the scrabbling sound, Eve opened her eyes to dimly see Adam sweeping the pavement for the elusive flashlight. "Got it." He flicked on the light as he squatted beside her once more. "Hold this," he commanded, thrusting it into her hand and angling the light on her leg.

Eve saw the dark blotch on her beige wool slacks even as she felt a trickle of warmth running down her leg. Adam stretched her leg out, her heel resting on the ground, and gently raised the hem of her pants leg above the middle of her calf. A lump had swollen across the middle of her leg, bisected by a gash from which blood ran freely.

"Looks worse than it is, though I'm sure it hurts like hell." Adam looked down at her and Eve released her bottom lip, which she had been worrying between her teeth. "You okay?"

"Yes. What a stupid thing to do."

"Not to worry. Let me get my bag, and I'll fix up a temporary bandage till we get home. I can take a better look at it there, but I don't think you're going to need stitches."

Adam left her side for a moment and returned with a huge black bag that he set down beside her. "I've got an idea. Can you shine that light over there by the corner of the building?" A wave of his hand indicated where he meant.

Digging into his pocket, he moved toward what turned out to

be an ice machine when Eve turned the flashlight in that direction. Pumping in coins, he returned with a five-pound plastic bag that he dropped by her leg. He took the flashlight to rummage inside his bag, dropped several packages on the pavement, then handed the light back to her as he set a bottle beside her leg and removed the cap.

Tearing open a package, he removed a square of gauze and liberally soaked it with liquid from the bottle. "This is Betadine. It's going to sting like the dickens, but it's necessary."

Eve inhaled a ragged breath as he cleaned her leg, leaving orangey-brown streaks. She felt a soothing coolness as he fanned his hand back and forth over the open cut. He tore open another package of gauze, folded it, and told her to hold it in place over the cut while he took the flashlight and rummaged in his bag once more. When he handed back the light, a plastic glove dangled between his teeth while he tore open the bag of ice. Dropping a couple of handfuls inside the glove, he stretched the end and tied it into a knot.

"Presto, an ice bag," Adam said with a grin. With care, he lifted her hand from the bandage, laid the impromptu ice bag on top, and replaced her hand. Tearing open yet another package, he began to wind gauze gently around her leg above and below her fingers. "Okay, you can take your hand away now." He finished securing the ice bag in place and looked up at her. "How are you holding out?"

She managed to smile in spite of the throbbing pain. "Very well, thank you. And I take back what I said about your bedside manner."

His mustache curled over a grin, but all he said was, "Sit tight while I clean up."

Scooping up the torn wrappers and bag of ice, he walked away, and a moment later Eve heard the clatter of ice cubes in a trash bin. Adam returned to close his bag and deposit it in the truck.

He stopped in front of her once more and said, "I'm going to take your hands and pull you up. Put all your weight on your right leg. Then I'll lift you and put you into the truck."

Eve let him pull her to a standing position, but when he released her, she put a restraining hand against the iron wall of his chest where his denim jacket hung open. "I'm sure I can hobble around and climb in myself."

She might as well have saved her breath. One second she was standing, and the next she was scooped up into his arms. Another man who knew better than she what was good for her.

"I assure you I'm perfectly capable of managing."

"Yes, but why should you? Just relax. You can be an independent city girl again tomorrow. For now, you follow doctor's orders, which means being still and letting others help you."

She stared at him in consternation, then sighed. Riding high against his chest, Eve curled an arm across his shoulder then rested her forehead against her arm, hiding the fact she was biting her lip against the pain that shot up her leg. But her nose was only inches away from Adam's open shirt collar and the distractingly pleasant odor of man, tobacco, and shaving lotion.

As he stepped carefully between the vehicles, he lowered his chin to see how to maneuver her body so that her leg didn't brush against the side of the truck. Eve inhaled deeply of his warm male scent just as his jaw grazed her lips, stubble scraping seductively across the damp moisture of her mouth, the softness of his mustache tickling her nose. A jolt raced through her, releasing a surprising flood of warmth deep within her body. She was surprised to find herself capable of physically responding to any man, especially after Richard's betrayal.

Adam felt the tightening of the small hand on his shoulder at the same moment his own grasp seemed to more closely gather the light burden in his arms. He paused unknowingly. His glance darted to Eve's slightly parted lips a hairs breadth away from his own. All he had to do was lower his head a fraction and he could taste the heavenly scent that had invaded his senses as soon as he'd picked her up.

Lordy, some days you couldn't win. One woman this evening had all but thrown herself at him and *he* wasn't interested. He wanted to sip of this woman's sweetness and sink slowly into her softness, and apparently *she* wasn't interested if her earlier comment could be believed. With an effort, Adam pulled his gaze from Eve's tantalizing lips and forced his legs to move.

He stopped beside the passenger door and had to clear his throat before he trusted his voice. "Just release the handle. You'll bump your leg if you try to pull the door open, so I'll elbow it aside."

She followed his instructions without looking at him. If he'd thought holding her was sweet torture, it was nothing compared to what followed after placing Eve on the seat. He had to slide his hands back under her body to adjust her position until he could raise her left leg to rest on the dashboard.

Adam slid behind the wheel with relief, glad to have something more solid than soft, scented female to hold onto. Soft, scented, *curvaceous* female, he amended. He pulled the truck onto the road carefully, glancing over at Eve. "You okay?"

"I'm fine."

He noticed she still hadn't looked at him, and he mentally swore at himself. She was in a difficult enough situation without adding his lust to her problems. Trying to distract her and get things back to normal, he asked, "How long's it been since you had a tetanus shot?"

Her head swiveled toward him at last. "About a year. Last spring, in fact."

"Good. If it turns out you need stitches after all, I'll take you to the emergency room after dinner."

"Couldn't you do it yourself? I mean, to save time and all. I'd be happy to pay you."

Adam turned his head and frowned at her briefly to let her know what she could do with her money before watching the road again. "I suppose I could, but it'd be more ethical to have a regular doctor do it."

"Why, what's your specialty?"

"My specialty, as you put it, happens to be four-footed critters rather than the two-legged kind."

Two

"You're a veterinarian?"

Grinning, Adam glanced at Eve's outraged expression. "It's a perfectly honorable profession."

"Yes, I know, but you just tended to my leg and—"

"A cut's a cut, whether you've got two legs or four."

"Yes, but—"

Adam chuckled; he couldn't help it. Immediately her sputtering broke off. When he glanced at her again, she was watching him suspiciously.

"What?" Eve demanded.

Struggling to contain the grin still stretched across his face, he admitted, "Your leg is much prettier than any horse's I've ever worked on."

A second of silence ticked by. Adam looked over in time to watch Eve's stiff expression relax into the smile she couldn't control. "I suppose I should be flattered," she said. "I mean, I've never been compared so favorably to a horse before."

He laughed outright. "There's a first time for everything."

"I have a feeling, Dr. Wagner, that my ego may suffer if I'm around you very long." Her tone was wryly amused.

"Adam," he reminded her, staring straight ahead.

And her ego couldn't suffer any more than his had. Her earlier remark still rankled. A chaperone eliminated any hint of reputations being compromised—for either of them. But damn it! She made it sound like she wasn't attracted to him enough for it to even be a consideration.

Eve wasn't quite sure what had happened, but her rescuer didn't seem quite so amused anymore. In fact, from what she could see in the dimly lit cab of the truck, he looked distinctly unhappy. Perhaps he thought she *had* disparaged his profession. Nothing could be further from the truth, of course; she'd just been surprised.

Without stopping to wonder why she even cared what Adam thought, she tried to relieve the droop of his mustache. "So what kind of animals do you care for? Farm animals?"

"Large and small. I'm the only veterinarian for some distance. I visit farms to see large animals in the morning and in the afternoon, I see small animals at my clinic in town."

"What about pets?"

He flashed a grin at her. "They're what's known as 'small animals' in the business."

"Oh." Undaunted, she said without thinking, "I wouldn't have thought that veterinarians work this late, especially on Saturdays." Realizing she might have presumed too much, Eve hurriedly added, "I'm sorry, I just realized you might not have been working after all."

"It was supposed to be an emergency. Turns out it was more social." A massive shrug accompanied his words, but Eve could tell he hadn't been pleased by whatever had happened.

Since he didn't volunteer any more, she left him to his own thoughts. She looked out the side window as they neared the end of the small town they'd been traveling through. A streetlight flooded an intersection just before the expanse of country darkness encroached once more.

They were almost past the intersection before the name she'd read on the street sign registered. She chuckled. "Why in the world would someone call a street Blood Lane?"

"Well, let me see if I remember." Adam's mustache danced in a ripple as he screwed up his mouth in thought. "I'd like to tell you it had something to do with a shootout in the 1800s, but actually it was named after a prominent family."

"The 1800s?" Eve let out a little breath of surprise. "Good grief, how old is the town?"

"Most of this area was settled around the same time as Chicago, so I'd say somewhere in the early 1830s." He grinned over at her. "If you think Blood Lane is weird, how about Frog Alley?"

Eve laughed. "In my valley, there's even one named The Haunt."

She smiled and said, "You mean in the valley where you live? Why is it called The Haunt?"

"Well, I do live in the valley, but I also own it." A deprecating roll of his shoulders tossed the information off. "As to why, there's a bog. In the old days, people used to think the dancing lights sometimes seen there were ghosts. So, The Haunt. Nowadays, of course, scientists tell us it's because of swamp gas. Takes all the fun away somehow."

She grinned and agreed with him. But impressed, she asked, "Do you really own a whole valley?"

"Just about, or I should say I own most of it outright. The bank and I share title to a couple of plots, and there's a few left that belong to outsiders."

"But why do you want to own a whole valley?"

"Sometimes I ask myself the same question." Adam's smile was rueful as he glanced at her. "At one time, the whole valley belonged to my family. My great-great-great-grandfather came here and homesteaded with his wife in 1830.

"My granddad had to sell off a few pieces during the depression and my father . . . sold some more before he died. Granddad made it his life's work to buy back that property. By the time he died last year, he'd managed to recover all but one of the pieces he'd sold and three of my dad's." Adam's shoulders twitched in the lazy roll she was beginning to recognize. "Since granddad raised me from the time I was ten years old, I sort of grew up expecting to do the same thing."

Eve had so many questions, she didn't know where to begin. But while pride had certainly tinged Adam's voice when talking about the property, she'd deciphered a note of sadness, too. She wondered how much his father had sold and if that might not be a touchy subject. Seeking the least offensive question, she finally said, "Just how big is this valley of yours?"

"About three miles by two miles, around fourteen hundred acres. We've been driving on my property since we turned off the main road."

For the first time, Eve realized they were traveling uphill. She waited quietly until they crested and then sighed with disappointment. It was too dark to see anything but the glow of lights from a house some distance away on one side of the valley. They started back down, their headlights flashing on groves of trees and black emptiness that might be fields. They'd traveled about halfway across the valley when they wound around a bend, and their lights flashed across a house.

"Whose home is that?"

"Belonged to one of those people my granddad bought out. There used to be several houses scattered throughout the valley, but we took down most of them to save on taxes."

They continued winding around the country lane on the floor of the valley. Sometimes Eve could see cultivated fields. She wondered how Adam found time to do any farming if he spent most of the day working as a veterinarian. Finally, she asked him.

"That's the problem, there's not enough time. But I have a manager and some farmhands. In fact," he looked over at Eve, "Carl, the manager who oversees all of our farms and orchards, is Sudie's husband. They live here in the valley, too. Besides ours, there's still one farm worked and lived on that my granddad sold.

One is worked by someone outside the valley, and two sit completely idle. The owner isn't interested in farming them."

The question rose naturally in Eve to ask whether they were perhaps for sale. But she left it unsaid. Either Adam couldn't afford to buy them back or they simply weren't on the market. Either way, she was sure it rankled that the farms were beyond his reach.

They began to climb almost immediately after a hairpin turn onto another road and they continued climbing, following the sharp curves in the road. Looking back carefully so as not to jar her leg, she could now see the lights of another house somewhere across the valley. Gradually the incline lessened. When they reached the crest the road continued on, but Adam turned off onto a driveway bordered by a screen of bushes. She'd expected a narrow, two-story farmhouse dwarfed by a barn. Instead, Eve saw a mammoth stone house with a car and a truck parked in one lane of the drive. They parked next to another car in an attached garage.

As he cut the ignition, Adam said, "Sudie's husband Carl is also here for dinner. Sit tight and I'll come around and get you." He left his Stetson on the seat.

Butterflies fluttered in Eve's stomach, and she wasn't sure if it was because of the thought of Adam carrying her again or facing the unknown Sudie and Carl.

He maneuvered her out of the truck and, to break the silence, she asked, "Does Sudie cook for you every night?"

"No. Usually she leaves something for me to reheat, but we were clearing a field today. With so many people to cook for, Sudie used the kitchen here. It's bigger than the one at her place."

They had reached the door into the house when it swung open. A small, plump, pink-cheeked woman stared at them in surprise. "Well, glory be! What happened?" She stood back so Adam could enter with Eve in his arms.

He walked through a laundry room into a huge kitchen and set Eve down at a table laid with two place settings. An older man, almost as tall as Adam and as strongly built, had risen at their appearance. But Eve had eyes for little except the man who had carried her in. She tried to study him without staring and was given an extra few moments as Adam raised her leg and slid a chair underneath to support it.

His large hands were gentle as he adjusted first her leg, then the chair, his concentration focused on settling her comfortably. The first thing Eve noticed was that Adam was suntanned and that his brown hair had been lightened on top by the sun to almost a honey color. In fact, she could see the bright overhead light reflecting on golden strands in his mustache. The hair at the back of his head curled over his collar, longer than she was used to seeing on the corporate types at work.

At the sudden tension in the hands still holding her leg, Eve's gaze switched to Adam's face. Hazel eyes, full of dark green and golden brown, stared back at her. Crinkly lines deepened at the corners of his eyes and, as he moved slightly, she took in his mustache that partially hid a smile.

"By the looks of you two, a body would think you'd never seen each other before."

Sudie chuckled at her own words, but looked amazed when Adam said, "Well, it's the first *good* look we've had, considering that it's dark as sin outside." He let his gaze sweep over Eve where she sat, warmed by his appreciative expression. "Sudie and Carl, this is Eve Sutton. She had a little run-in with the truck hitch when we dropped her car off. I'll take another look at her injury after we've eaten." He waved a hand to include both people hovering around the table. "Sudie and Carl Bergen."

Carl ducked his head, but Sudie apparently acted as spokesperson for both of them. "We're glad to make your acquaintance, Eve. I'm just sorry you're having such a time of it this evening." She stood beside Eve, hands planted on the sides of her plump, apron-covered hips, wagging her head from side to side. "Let's get some food inside you and maybe you won't looked so peaked. Adam, you go wash up and I'll give Eve a damp cloth."

Sudie shooed him away as she charged over to a huge double sink, yanked off some paper towels and wet them. She was back with the warm, wet towels before Adam even cleared the room. Eve took them with grateful thanks, lost in amusement as she studied the housekeeper's quick, bird-like movements. So she looked "peak-ed," did she, unconsciously mimicking Sudie's expression. Compared to the suntanned faces of the others, she supposed she did.

"We've already eaten, of course," Sudie informed her as she turned off a burner, "but it won't take but two shakes of a lamb's tail to get yours ready. Carl, you might as well sit down and take a load off. I'll chat with them for a few minutes, then go home with you to gather my things for tonight."

She continued putting dinner on the table, smiling when she happened to cross gazes with Eve. Adam returned just as she set glasses of iced tea on the table and asked, "So where're you from?"

"Chicago." Barely were the words out of her mouth before Eve realized from Sudie's expectant look that she was supposed to divulge more of her background.

Heavens! What could she say? She certainly didn't want to tell them about the real Evelyn Sutton, and she hadn't had time to consider what she was going to tell anyone about the new Eve. She took a hasty sip of iced tea to give herself a few moments.

Sudie tipped her head and inquired, "You visiting someone in the area?"

"Now, Mother," Carl laid a hand on Sudie's arm, "it's not polite to badger someone with questions."

"Badger? Who's badgering? If a body don't ask questions, how's someone supposed to know they're interested?" Sudie's bird-like gaze returned to Eve.

It was impossible to take offense at someone who looked like a plump, inquisitive robin. Eve smiled slightly to let them know she didn't mind and said the first thing that came to mind. "I've taken a leave of absence from work for a month." That much at least was true.

Adam interrupted the grilling to ask, "Is there someone you should call to let them know you've been detained? If so, feel free to use the phone."

Eve shook her head. "No, thanks anyway. I'm sure I'll be on my way again tomorrow."

"Well, as to that . . ." He propped an elbow on the table and brushed absently at his mustache with a thumb.

Her gaze followed his slow strokes against the satiny texture, then blinked, realizing his hesitation obviously did not bode well for her plans. With a slight groan, she remembered. "Farm country, right?"

"Right." His grin took in Sudie and Carl. "For a city girl, she's quick." His grin became rueful, however, as he turned back to

Eve. "I'm afraid the service station is closed on Sundays. People tend to take the Good Book literally around here."

"But I can't impose upon you—"

"It's not an imposition."

"And I don't mind spending the nights here," Sudie added. "It'll be nice to have another woman to talk to for a change. Besides," she turned and smiled impishly at Carl beside her, "it'll do him good to miss me a little." Carl blushed and ducked his head before a smile warmed his stern features. Sudie turned back to the table, then stared in surprise. "Glory be! I'm standing here jawing and your dinner is getting cold. Pass me those plates."

A heaping dish of stew was set before Eve. As the delicious aroma of steaming potatoes, carrots, celery, tomatoes, and beef wafted to her, she realized she was famished. Liberally buttering a huge piece of cornbread, she dug into the food with relish as Carl filled Adam in on what had transpired in his absence. The details of their discussion about planting the new field and Adam's translation to her carried them through dessert. Carl and Sudie joined them for huge slices of apple pie and coffee.

The warmth of the kitchen, her full tummy, and the mostly sleepless night before made Eve drowsy. She literally jumped when Sudie snapped her fingers.

"In all the excitement I almost forgot. I have to find someone to replace Alice Rasmussen at the fair tomorrow." At Adam's puzzled look, Sudie explained, "She cut her hand, poor thing, when she was fixing dinner today. Needed stitches. Though where I'm going to find an artist at this late date is beyond me."

"An artist?" Eve pulled herself erect in the chair, fully awake now. If there was some way she could repay these people for all their trouble. . . . "What do you need an artist for?"

"It's the spring planting fair. Alice had volunteered to paint the little children's faces. You know, rainbows and pretty things for the girls and spiders and such for the boys."

Eve smiled in relief. Such a task was certainly within her capability. In meetings with the advertising and PR people, she'd always been able to sketch her ideas for them to work up with an agency artist. "I'd be happy to fill in for her if you'll let me. Only," her smile dimmed a little, "I don't know how I'm going to get where I'm supposed to be since my car is out of action."

Sudie chuckled. "That's an easy one to solve. We're all going to the fair. I'll call Alice and tell her we'll pick up the art supplies on our way in tomorrow morning. And thanks, you're a lifesaver."

The housekeeper rose and started clearing the table as Eve said, "It's I who should thank all of you. I don't know what I would have done if Dr. Wagner hadn't come along."

"Adam," he reminded her.

Eve shifted on the chair and winced when she tried to move her leg.

Sudie, gathering up the cups and saucers, saw her expression. "If your leg is still bothering you tomorrow, I'll volunteer Carl's services to tote you around the fairgrounds."

"That won't be necessary." Adam leaned back in his chair with a smile. "I've sort of got the knack of carrying her around by now. I'll do it."

Eve shifted on the chair again, uncomfortable at the amused glance Sudie sent her as the housekeeper reached the sink to finish washing the last dishes.

She was grateful for the change in subject when Carl said, "What was wrong with Wind Dancer this afternoon?"

At the reminder of his wild goose chase, Adam felt his smile slip. "Nothing a good tanning of Jane Hartwig's backside by her father wouldn't cure." At Carl's startled look and Sudie's tisking admonition from the sink, he explained, "That's why I was so late tonight. Jane said she'd left Wind Dancer in one of the far pastures, hadn't wanted to move her. I should have known then something was up. Emery Hartwig wouldn't leave one of his prize race horses out in *any* pasture if something was wrong with it. I just wasn't thinking."

Bracing an elbow on the table, he rubbed a practiced thumb over his mustache as he tried to dampen his anger. "Anyway, we drove out there, just Jane and I. When I couldn't find anything wrong, she acted full of surprise that the horse could have recovered so quickly. When I pressed her for symptoms, she began to trip herself up with contradictory statements." He sighed. "I'm afraid I lost my temper and confronted her with her little subterfuge. For my stupidity, I got to walk all the way back to the house after Jane took off in my truck."

Silence reigned for a few moments. Carl looked worried. Then

Sudie, her hands still warm and damp, rested them along with the dishtowel on his shoulders. "Adam," she began tentatively, "Emery Hartwig is a powerful man in these parts. I know Jane's a thorn in your side, but don't you think you should—"

"No, Sudie. There's no way I'm going to kowtow to that man. Or his daughter. I'm tired of Emery and others like him throwing their weight around, thinking their wealth gives them the right to do whatever they damn well please." An uncomfortable but not unsympathetic silence followed.

Sudie squeezed his shoulders. "Come on, Carl. You get his bag so he can tend to Eve's leg." She wandered away, and Adam heard the clink of china and silver as she put things away.

Adam's abstracted gaze had fastened on a bright, shining glow in the reflection of the overhead wrought-iron chandelier. His thoughts weren't pleasant, centered as they were around Hartwig and his spoiled daughter. One of his granddad's expressions came to him: As the twig is bent, so grows the tree. He nearly snorted. What did he expect when Jane's father gratified her every whim? It just galled him that Hartwig didn't have better sense, especially for someone in his position.

The shining haze in front of Adam shifted and he blinked, focusing on the bright, smooth cap of Eve's blond hair that brushed her shoulders. His gaze lowered to her pale face. She returned his stare with a slight crease marring the smoothness of her forehead.

His attention sharpened. "You look worried about something. What is it?"

Eve's head dipped, making the long swing of her hair from the side part hide half her face. She hesitated so long, he was beginning to wonder if she was going to answer when she said, "I just realized I don't know anything about the people I'm likely to meet tomorrow. In fact, I know nothing about this area at all. Perhaps it was presumptuous of me to offer to fill in. Maybe I won't come up to your standards. Or theirs."

"There's nothing for you to worry about. The only people you have to worry about pleasing are aged ten and under. Just showing up is going to make them happy."

Eve raised her head at his reassurance, and he read a slight lessening of the tension in her expression. Something still bothered her though and, after thinking about it, he added, "The people are a mix of farmers and those who live here, but commute to Madison, Milwaukee and other towns to work. They're just everyday people like you'd meet anywhere. They won't be expecting Michelangelo." Adam grinned. "Besides, they wouldn't have gotten that with Alice anyway."

"What about people like your Mr. Hartwig?"

"He's not my anything. I wouldn't have him on a bet."

"I meant—Sudie said he's someone of considerable importance in the area. What does he do?"

"Besides owning a large portion of the county, he's the president of the local bank."

Adam couldn't help the slight tensing of his shoulders when talking about Hartwig; he didn't like the man and never had. Eve's clear blue gaze bored into his, and he felt as if she could see into his mind. Trying to divert her, he continued, "The only connection Hartwig has to the fair is handing out ribbons at the races and eventually handing over a check from the proceeds to the F.F.A."

Eve's face was an open book. Clearly mystified by the initials, her eyebrows arched. He kept forgetting she was a city girl. "Future Farmers of America," he explained.

Carl entered just as Sudie finished with the dishes and came over to stand by Eve. Her husband joined her at the table, setting the black bag down by Adam, and put an arm around Sudie. "You want me to get your things for you and bring them back here?"

"No, thanks. It'll take less time to get them myself. I'll be back before Adam and Eve are fin—" Sudie's expression was one of blank astonishment as she broke off and turned to stare first at Adam, then Eve. A ripple of merry laughter followed.

"Oh, my," she said, patting her chest, "that's wonderful. Adam and Eve." She broke out in laughter again, and Adam found himself joining in her merriment. Even the reserved Carl could be heard chuckling. Eve's face gradually relaxed in a small smile.

Sudie continued laughing. As she went out the door, her words floated back. "Adam and Eve."

Three

Adam still shared a smile with Eve as Sudie and Carl left, though they'd have to be careful with their teasing. He didn't want her to feel uncomfortable with their names being linked.

He said, "I'd better take a look at your leg before that makeshift ice bag starts to leak." Gathering a bowl filled with warm water and a few pieces of paper towel, he placed them on the table and moved his bag beside Eve. "I'm going to have to shift you away from the table so I have some room to work."

Adam repositioned her and settled into another chair. While he dug in the bag at his feet for his scissors, he admired the curve of Eve's exposed leg since her pant leg was still rolled above the bandage. The size of the package might be small, but there was nothing wrong with the contents.

To allay any anxiety Eve might be having about her injury, he distracted her as he unwound the bandage. "It was nice of you to offer to fill in tomorrow. Is that what you do? I mean, are you an artist?"

"No, though I suppose I might have been if I'd been allowed to study what I wanted to in college."

"So what did you wind up doing? Wait, let me guess." Adam looked up, his hands stilled momentarily, as he gazed into blue eyes that reminded him of the purplish-blue lobelia his grand-mother had been so fond of. With a straight face, he said, "You run an import business specializing in tropical fish because there's a huge demand for exotic fish to fill all those yuppie aquariums." When Eve chuckled, he frowned. "No? Hmmm."

Adam remembered the white square in the rear window of her car, correctly having identified it as an application for license plates. Since she had bought a used car, she obviously didn't have much money. He wondered what she did for a living that would allow her to take a month's leave of absence.

He removed the rubber glove now filled with only cool water. Soaking the blood-encrusted gauze that covered her wound, he continued in an outrageous vein. "Since this is the age of feminism, how about this? You're a successful businesswoman who makes piles of money and runs circles around your executives."

The tensing of her muscles in his hands told Adam he had struck some kind of nerve, but he kept his gaze on his hands as he gently lifted away the gauze. Turning Eve's leg from side to side to see the extent of damage, he finally said, "No cigar, huh? Okay, I give. Tell me what you do."

"It's no big deal, I assure you." Her voice was cool, somewhat clipped. "I'm just a small cog in the office wheel of an electronics firm. There are at least a dozen people in the office who are as capable as I am at what I do."

Reaching into his bag once more, Adam removed the Betadine solution and more gauze. "So why couldn't you study art like you wanted to in college?"

"Because my father wanted me to be prepared for the real world, as he called it."

Adam opened the bottle of antiseptic and glanced at her. "I take it there were no brothers for him to push?" Eve shook her head, the smooth strands of her hair swinging to and fro around her shoulders. "Well, I guess it never hurts to be able to support yourself. Of course, without him ever giving you the chance to find out, you'll never know whether you might have made it as an artist. Or do you paint in your spare time?" He looked up from cleaning her leg.

"No, there's never enough time."

"Too bad. The world can always use more beauty."

He worked in silence for awhile, wondering how he'd considered Eve rather bland when he first met her. In regular lighting, there was no question Eve Sutton was damned fetching—especially when she smiled.

"Will I need stitches?"

"No, I'm going to use butterfly bandages to hold the edges of the wound together. Of course, that means you're going to have to stay off your feet and keep that leg propped up, at least through tomorrow."

Adam carefully pushed the edges of the wound together and affixed the first of several tiny bandages. "You're going to have a small scar there that will take some time to fade."

"I think my vanity can take it." Eve smiled and, just the way she shrugged his comment off, he knew she placed little value on her looks.

Finished taping the butterfly-shaped plastic strips in place, he rose and put away his paraphernalia. "How about if I lug you into the living room? It's cool enough for a fire, and I think a glass of wine would relax you." He turned from disposing of the old bandage and caught her deepening smile as he stooped to pick her up and carry her into the next room. "What's so funny?"

"You are." Eve linked her hands about his shoulder and neck, realizing he had to be in terrific shape to lift her so effortlessly. As he carried her through a hall with pegged floors, she deliberately made her voice light and teasing. "You had me fooled at first with your . . . colloquial expressions, but I've discovered you use them as cover."

Adam looked down at her with an arched brow and a look of . . . what? Discomfort that she had hit the mark so closely? "Well, you do," she insisted with a grin. "If you want to play the part of a country doctor, excuse me, a country veterinarian, then you have to stay in character, not slip up and let people know how up-to-date you are."

He deposited her gently on one of a pair of facing sofas before a huge fieldstone fireplace. "Saw right through me, huh?"

"Those yuppie aquariums gave you away."

He grinned down at her, his hands resting on his slim hips, though slim was a relative term considering his size. Viewing one of his legs cocked at an angle, Eve followed the powerful outline of his thigh down to the tip of his boot. The heels of his cowboy boots might add an inch to his height, but Adam had to stand more than six feet without any help at all.

Realizing she was staring, Eve shifted her gaze and made a production of patting the orange-brown antiseptic streaks adorning her calf to make sure her leg was dry. She unrolled the bunched wool above her wound and lowered her leg to the faded sofa.

Adam had walked over to an antique dry sink and removed a bottle of wine. She glanced around the huge room and took in the rest of the furnishings. Like the sofa, most of the upholstered pieces and drapes were a bit faded, but their muted rust and gold tones only made the room more appealing. No decorating had been done for some time, but the furniture had obviously been expensive to begin with and had held up well.

In the quiet, Adam's boots echoed on the pegged floor before he reached the area rug. He handed Eve a heavy lead crystal goblet filled with a ruby-red wine and set his down on the mammoth coffee table between the sofas. Wordlessly, he dropped to one knee on the fireplace apron and lit the kindling under logs laid in preparation. It wasn't long before leaping flames joined the soft lamplight to create a rosy glow.

Adam picked up his glass and settled on the sofa opposite her. Raising his glass in a silent salute, he sipped the dry, slightly tart wine, then rested the footed stem on his stomach as he leaned back on the cushion. "So what are you going to do with your month's leave?"

"Nothing much." She turned the goblet in her hand, enjoying the dancing light reflected from the crackling fire in its myriad facets. "Just rest and relaxation as I try to figure out what I'm going to do with the rest of my life."

"Sounds like a heavy load for 'nothing much.' Want to talk about it?"

"I didn't mean to make it sound so complicated." Eve shrugged and studied her wineglass. "My father died about a year ago and, since I just broke off my engagement, I guess I'm trying to find a new direction." Looking into the fire, she continued, "The life my father laid out for me lacks . . . fulfillment, I guess, for want of a better term. I don't feel the sense of accomplishment I thought I would." Glancing at Adam, she smiled. "So I've given myself permission to try and figure out what would make me happy."

Her freedom pleased him. "And where're you going to do this?"

"A cabin on a lake about an hour north of here."

Adam drank some more wine and realized he was willing to

do everything in his power to make sure Eve wanted to stick around for awhile. He had an idea, but didn't want to seem pushy.

"Tell you what. Why don't you see how you like the area tomorrow? If you're comfortable with things, you could stay in my granddad's house. It's just down the road." Grinning to cover a sudden nervousness, he said, "Why should you pay rent when you can get it free? Unless, of course, you've already paid a deposit?"

Eve shook her head, but the way her gaze slid by his, he could tell she was wary. Hell, why shouldn't she be? He'd just met her two hours ago and already he was trying to tie her down. Though he'd been delighted to learn she was free of emotional entanglements, his last thought jerked him into caution.

"It's just a suggestion. You don't have to decide now. Besides," Adam said with sudden realization, "we don't know what's wrong with your car. You may be stuck with us a few days anyway, depending upon the problem." Eve smiled back at him, and he relaxed.

"Is your grandfather's house smaller than this?"

"Much smaller, so you wouldn't have to worry about spending all your time cleaning. Hey, maybe you could pass the time painting. If you wanted to, that is. And there's a small lake tucked in one end of the valley if you want to swim."

He swallowed some more wine, trying to think of things she might like to do that would tempt her to stay. "Do you ride? I can offer you a mount."

"Yes, but there hasn't been much time for it in recent years." Eve tilted her head and looked thoughtful. "What do you do for fun?"

Adam pulled one booted foot across his knee and swirled the wine in his glass. "You're probably not going to believe this, but on the rare occasions when I can find a chunk of time I like to go sailing."

"Your lake or Lake Michigan?"

"Lake Michigan. I've got a small cutter I fool around in." It seemed like too much to hope for, but he asked anyway. "You sail?"

"I was practically raised on the water. My father loved it."

Then she looked at him with curiosity. "How did a landlocked farmer-veterinarian discover sailing?"

"I won a sunfish in a contest as a teenager. Used our lake as a learning ground."

"Do you still have it?"

"Yeah, I do. It's stored in my granddad's barn. Maybe if nothing else, we can take it out one day while you're here."

Adam was about to explore other possible interests when a familiar howl went up by the kitchen door. At Eve's startled look, he reassured her. "Relax. It's just Sheba, my dog."

He went to let in the collie, who gave an excited bark as he approached the door to the garage. She wriggled with joy as she greeted him.

Adam found some burrs in her fur and scolded, "You've been out cattin' around again, haven't you? Oh no, you don't." Sheba already had her nose to the ground and was about to bound out of the laundry room as he reached for her brush. "We're going to smarten you up. Can't have you meeting a lady when you look like you've been pulled through a bush backward. Hold still."

When he reentered the living room with the dog at his heels, Adam hesitated a moment to enjoy the picture of Eve resting with her head on the back of the sofa, her blond hair spilling over the cushion. He'd been out of the room a matter of five minutes, yet he had a sense of coming home. The image of Eve waiting for him in this room at the end of a long day with a welcoming fire and glass of wine leaped to a further image: the two of them stretched before the fire, entwined in each other's arms.

Sheba deserted his side and padded to the sofa. He probably shouldn't be surprised, judging by his own reaction a moment ago. Though she usually didn't approach strangers, Sheba was obviously as taken with Eve as he was. He'd always considered animals a better judge of people than most humans; it was nice to have his impression of Eve confirmed. The dog sat quietly and offered a paw while he wondered if he'd convinced her to stick around.

Lack of sleep and the warmth of the fire, combined with the wine and dinner, had so relaxed Eve that her eyelids slid closed despite her efforts to keep them open. Drifting in a drowsy state, she heard Adam's returning footsteps and the click of a dog's nails on the floor. She had to sit up; she would any second now.

She felt the slight dip of a touch on the cushion and opened her eyes with difficulty. A beautiful black, tan and cream collie sat poised in front of the sofa, her paw hovering over the cushion. Sheba, that was her name. Drawing herself up, Eve stretched to shake the dog's paw. As soon as she did, Sheba moved next to her, edging the elegant length of her aristocratic nose beneath Eve's hand.

"Oh, you're a lovely girl." She ran her hand over the satiny head. Immediately, a tongue lapped at her and Eve leaned over to embrace the animal.

"Looks like a mutual admiration," Adam said from the sofa across from her, his mustache curved over his smile.

"She's beautiful." Eve drew her fingers through the fluffy ruff of cream-colored fur at Sheba's throat. "What—"

Sheba let loose with a soft woof at the same moment headlights flashed across the room. Adam put down his wineglass again and rose, saying, "Must be Sudie. I'll bring in the suitcases, and she can get you settled for bed. You look like you're half asleep."

Sheba remained by her side, even after Adam returned and carried her case and that of his housekeeper's upstairs. Sudie bustled in, offering her a snack before retiring.

"I don't know where I'd put it," Eve replied, stroking Sheba's sleek coat. "Thanks for the wonderful dinner and for playing musical beds."

The cheery woman waved a hand at her, then propped her hands on her hips. "Well, if that don't beat all. I've never seen Sheba take to anyone like she has you. Besides Adam, that is." The collie chose that moment to lay her head on the cushion next to Eve, looking up at her with adoring eyes while her plume of a tail waved gently.

"Looks like you've made a friend for life," Adam said, stepping next to the sofa. He moved the dog out of the way and leaned over. "Bedtime."

He scooped Eve up before she had a chance to protest, then she was distracted by Sheba's excited barking as the dog danced in circles around them. "Down, girl. Quiet." The collie immediately obeyed his command, but whined as she watched them.

With Eve's hands linked behind his neck, she felt the movement of Adam's firm muscles as he turned his head to look down at her. Up close, she could see more than a sprinkling of golden strands in that tantalizing mustache. She remembered its softness brushing her skin earlier and swallowed at the reminder.

Adam's eyes were full of amusement as he said, "I think she's jealous." He looked beyond Eve to the still-whining dog. "If anyone here should be miffed, it's me. Some watchdog you are, making up to a stranger. You're a fickle female, Sheba." She just cocked her head and whined.

They all trooped up the stairs, Adam carrying Eve, Sheba on his heels, followed by a chuckling Sudie. He deposited Eve on the bed in a pleasant room and tried to evict the dog, but Sheba lay down on the braided rug and ignored him.

Leaning over to pat her head, Eve said, "I don't mind if she stays. If it's okay with you?" She looked up in time to catch the bemused expression on his face.

"No, it's all right." He turned at the door and said, "I just figured out that Sheba was jealous because *your* attention had been distracted from *her*. Talk about biting the hand that feeds you!"

Fondling the dog's ear, Eve grinned. "We women have to stick together."

"That's what I'm afraid of." Adam closed the door with a rueful smile as Sudie joined her chuckle.

The older woman found Eve's nightgown and robe in the suitcase and laid them across the bed. While she undressed, Sudie put away the rest of her clothes. They made the trek to the bathroom, Sudie offering her arm for support, with Sheba padding along after them. When Eve finished preparing for bed, she opened the bathroom door to find the collie lying across the doorway waiting for her.

Sudie said, "I don't think we're going to be able to pry her away from your side. Here, let me help."

Eve had tried not to limp, but after standing up for awhile her leg was throbbing. The housekeeper scooted next to her and took most of Eve's weight off her injured leg as they made their way back to the bedroom. She gratefully accepted Sudie's help getting into bed.

The housekeeper picked up her slacks, examining the tear in one leg. "They're ruined," Eve said, settling back against the plumped pillows.

"No, I don't think so. The cleaners should be able to get the blood out and, since the pants are wool, they can send them out to be rewoven. Wouldn't be worth it though unless the pants were expensive to start with." The housekeeper ran a critical eye over the material. "Looks like these cost a pretty penny."

Before Eve lost her courage, she said, "Sudie, I wanted to ask about something mentioned earlier, but I—I don't want to pry."

The older woman finished her inspection and turned toward the bed. Eve felt the heat rising in her cheeks and was grateful when Sudie lowered herself to the end of the bed with an encouraging smile.

"I'll be happy to answer any questions you have. Just relax and spit it out."

Her cheeks still warm, Eve said, "It's really none of my business, but I wondered about that man, Hartwig. Did he do something to Adam to cause such enmity or does Adam dislike all wealthy people for some reason?"

Sudie's expression had grown thoughtful. "By now, Adam probably equates wealth with people like Hartwig. And I guess he has reason to." She sighed. "Though I wondered tonight if he's not setting himself up for a fall. He's usually more open-minded and forgiving, but as I said, with Hartwig. . . ."

The housekeeper seemed to lose herself in reverie for a few moments. Animation returned as she cocked her head. "You'd never guess they're related, would you?"

Eve sat up straighter. "What?"

"Well, by marriage anyway. Adam's mother died before he started school, and his father—Drew—thought he should remarry for the boy's sake. Emery's sister caught his eye and, before Drew had time to blink, he found himself engaged.

"To make a long story short, Frances resembled her niece Jane in that she was spoiled. She and Drew hadn't been married a month before her complaints started about the cramped house, having to drive around in a truck, and more of the same dribble. And Emery didn't help none.

"Of course, they were used to the best, and he didn't see any reason why his sister couldn't continue to live in the same lifestyle in which she'd been raised. I guess they assumed because the Wagners owned this whole valley, or had, that they were as rich as the Hartwigs."

Sudie shook her head. "They weren't, of course. Most of their money went back into their farm and orchards and, when they could, buying back the property old Ramsey—Adam's grandfather—had to sell during the depression. So, they went from not owing anybody a cent and having the most advanced farm and machinery to more straightened circumstances as Drew kept going into debt to appease Frances."

Her gaze drifted around the room as she said, "He built her this big house." With her usual cheerfulness subdued by her sober tale, Sudie suddenly looked much older. "The end result was that Drew borrowed against the value of the property to finance this home, the furnishings, and a lot of other things Frances and Emery insisted she needed to make her happy."

Almost afraid to ask, Eve said, "What happened? Adam explained on the way here this evening that several pieces of the valley are owned by others, so—" She broke off as realization hit. "Oh, no! I just made the connection between Adam's comment about Hartwig being a banker and—Don't tell me it was his bank."

"Not only was it his bank," Sudie's rueful expression hardened, "but he was the one who snapped up the mortgages when the loans were called in."

"But why?"

"Because after Frances was killed in an auto accident, he saw no reason to continue to grant extensions on the loans." Eve's expression must have reflected her horror because Sudie reached over and patted her foot where it bulged under the quilt. "Not only did Drew die in the same accident, but it was the beginning of a string of bad luck.

"That summer, a farm hand was seriously injured, and Ramsey discovered Drew had let their insurance lapse. He bore the expense of two serious operations to save the man's leg. Then we had several years of long, hard winters alternating with two years of drought. There was only so much the old man could do."

Her voice was grim as she added, "But the final blow was

when Emery sold off all but two of the farms. While he held title to them, there was a chance to eventually buy them back. He's not interested in farming. To him, they were simply an investment. But the others . . . well, the property could be passed on to the owner's family and the Wagners might never have a chance of recovering it. And that's precisely what's happened to one farm. The Stoffels come from a large family, and it's been passed on twice already to relatives."

Sitting forward with her arms wrapped around her raised, quilt-covered knee, Eve said, "I bet Hartwig owns those two pieces of land that Adam said sit idle, doesn't he?"

"Yes, although Adam's made several offers to buy the property. But Emery doesn't appear to be in any hurry to get rid of it. Ramsey and Adam were able to develop relationships with the other owners and get first bid on the farms as they came on the market. The Frankels, who live here in the valley, are about ready to pack it in. Their children are scattered across the country and, like a lot of youngsters these days, aren't interested in farming. So they're no problem, and even the Stoffels have agreed to give Adam first refusal if they ever decide to sell. Emery is the only holdout. He won't agree to anything."

"He sounds like a very disagreeable person." Eve wrinkled her nose. She hoped she didn't run into him tomorrow; she didn't know if she could disguise her dislike all that well. Smothering a yawn, she said, "Thanks for taking the time to explain it all."

Sudie rose, chuckling. "Carl says I can talk the hind leg off a mule. I've enjoyed it, but I'd better go." She rose and smoothed the corner of the bed where she'd been sitting. "I'll have lots of time to fill you in on some other people you're likely to meet tomorrow morning before we leave. Get some sleep now."

Eve snapped off the lamp as Sudie left and slid down into the bed. Exhaustion overrode thoughts about what Adam's house-keeper had just told her, and her eyes drifted shut as she thought about being in his house.

Adam. Adam and Eve. She chuckled in the dark, remembering Sudie's glee at the coupling of their names. Her smile slipped though as she recalled her response to Adam in his arms after her accident. And again, just a short while ago. Could she blame the wine and the warmth of the room for the way she had bonelessly melted against him? It had felt so . . . right, so deliciously reasonable.

She decided it was probably a good thing Adam didn't like wealthy people. There was no place for a man in her life. She had more important things to do.

Four

Eve came awake slowly the next morning, disoriented because she didn't recognize her surroundings. Memory returned before she moved her legs, however. Pushing herself up in bed, she enjoyed the room's charm. Sunlight peeped from the edges of the pulled-down shades and brightened the faded wallpaper.

She looked over the side of the bed, but no dog lay curled on the braided rug. Someone had let Sheba out.

"Oh, good," Sudie said, opening the door a crack. "You're awake."

Eve smiled and threw back the covers. "Is it very late?" Gingerly, she lowered the foot of her injured leg to the floor.

"Goodness, no." Sudie bustled into the room with a tray containing a small china pot that smelled of fresh coffee. She set it on the dresser, saying, "But I didn't want you to have to rush. Would you like some help?"

Placing a hand on the nightstand, Eve stood on her good leg. "Let's see how I do on my own." It hurt when she took a step. She leaned over and raised the hem of her nightgown. If possible, her leg looked worse today. "Beautiful blue and purple colors, don't you think?"

"Not half as pretty as when the rest of the rainbow shows up." Sudie chuckled and followed her progress as she slipped into her robe and took a few tentative steps toward the door. "Want to try it by yourself?"

Eve nodded. But by the time she'd had a quick shower and returned to her room, she gratefully accepted Sudie's help. The housekeeper piled pillows behind her back and raised her legs onto the freshly made bed.

"I thought it might be too much for you, but it's always best to let people find out for themselves." When Eve settled with a sigh, Sudie brought over the tray and poured a cup of coffee. "There's cream and sugar if you want.

"Since the weather's still somewhat cool, I'd suggest slacks with a blouse and a nice warm sweater you can remove later if it gets too warm. Why don't you tell me what you want, and I'll get them for you? Then I'll finish straightening the other rooms. Just give me a call down the stairs when you're ready."

Eve considered her wardrobe and mentioned her last good pair of wool slacks, thanking the housekeeper for her help. She hadn't brought many nice clothes because she'd planned to rough it at the cabin.

She sipped her coffee as Sudie retrieved the clothes she wanted from the beautiful cherry wood Queen Anne chest of drawers. Studying the matching dressing table on the other side of the room and the nightstand next to her, Eve remembered the antique pieces strewn throughout the house. No veneers anywhere. Adam's stepmother might have been spoiled, but she'd had wonderful—if expensive—taste.

Even the oblique thought of Adam made Eve pause as she pulled off her nightgown. Had she really felt what she'd thought she had last night? Shaking her head, she reached for a periwinkle blue silk blouse at the end of the bed. For someone known for her practicality, she'd been acting pretty bizarre the last twenty-four hours.

Eve pulled on warm socks and slate-colored slacks, then reached for a matching cable stitched sweater. She reminded herself that this was a new day as she hobbled to the dressing table. Assured of her anonymity, she was determined to enjoy her freedom; she planned to live each day to its fullest for the next month. No more schedules, no more goals. And no more men, including the good doctor. She had no responsibilities, except to try to rediscover herself as she put her life back together and her self-improvement plan into action.

Staring at her pale reflection in the dressing-table mirror, Eve wished nature had been more generous. She applied makeup, considering her forehead too high, her nose a trifle too long, and her jaw too broad for real beauty. The only things she had going for her to balance those features were large expressive blue eyes with brows and lashes of a much darker color than her hair that fell somewhere between light ash brown and several shades of blonde. And her mouth, though she secretly thought it too wide, seemed to balance the rest of her face.

She applied makeup sparingly, but professionally. Outlining her lips, she told herself she at least had good teeth and a pretty complexion. Not much, all told, compared to wishing she looked like society's current vision of beauty. Her money though, had assured the best advice on makeup, hairstyle, and how to dress to make the most of the assets and small stature that nature had bestowed. Eve ran a brush through her hair, grateful for its natural curl, and hobbled to the top of the stairs.

Rather than bother Sudie, she decided to make her own way down. Easier said than done, even supporting her weight on the stair rails. So she sat on the top step and eased herself down to the next one, all the way to the first floor.

"Well, glory be!" Sudie said, appearing in the kitchen doorway after apparently hearing Eve's uneven step in the hall. "You must be one determined lady."

"Just hungry."

"Well, sit yourself down and I'll join you for a cup of coffee."

She decided that bustling must be Sudie's usual mode of movement. The woman had rarely paused last night or this morning. Now she whipped up scrambled eggs and removed hash browns, bacon and toast from a warm oven, making the transfer to the table in two easy trips.

Eve hadn't heard the deep drone of a male voice this morning, let alone seen Adam or Carl. Since there was only one place setting on the table, she said, "All that food for me? Where is everyone?"

"Adam left a note that he'd been called out to Jensens' before dawn. Their prize cow delivered recently. Something must have gone wrong with her. And Carl's making the rounds, checking on things. He'll be along soon. If Adam's not back in time, we can manage without him."

Eve deliberately ignored the pang she felt at Sudie's news and concentrated on her words. She hadn't realized exactly what a veterinarian's life would entail, she realized as she pulled up another chair to rest her throbbing leg on. Though she'd never seen a live cow, Sudie's words created an image of a gentle animal with huge, deer-like eyes. The thought of the animal in pain upset her. "Will she die?"

"Not if Adam can help it," Sudie said, sitting down opposite her.

Reassured more by her demeanor than her words, Eve asked, "Does that happen often, getting called out in the middle of the night?"

The housekeeper chuckled. "Dawn's not exactly the middle of the night, but come spring Adam's sleep is interrupted a great deal.

"Glad to see you're hungry." She smiled at Eve's evident enjoyment of the meal. "You look a little thin to me. Maybe if you're here a few days, we can put some weight on you."

Though her gaze flicked to Sudie's well-upholstered figure, Eve didn't say anything. She weighed exactly what she had in college, yet she probably should weigh more since she'd recently turned thirty. If she kept eating like she had since arriving here last night, no doubt she would. She shoved that thought, and lost dreams, aside for now.

Her appetite somewhat appeased, Eve asked Sudie to tell her about the spring planting fair and who she'd likely meet.

"Well, let's see. First off, you'll meet Alice Rasmussen when we pick up her supplies." Appraising her, Sudie said, "I'd say she's about your age. She's a dear, though I think she may have bitten off more than she can comfortably chew right now. Right after she opened her store, she discovered she was pregnant, so she's got her hands full with a business, teaching, and the new baby. Cutting her hand is really going to put a crimp in her schedule, even with Gladys's help."

"Who's Gladys?"

"Gladys Kopfman. Helps Alice out in the afternoons at the store and keeps an eye on the baby there until Alice finishes teaching at the school around three.

"The whole town turns out for the fair. People we've known forever and who are friends. Connie Hummel is an interior designer, her husband Jim runs the local insurance agency. Clarel Krpan is an accountant. Her husband is some corporate muckety-muck in Milwaukee. Otto Niehoff owns the local supermarket. His wife Frieda sits on just about every committee in town, as well as Caroline, Emery Hartwig's wife. There's a constant battle between the two of them to see who gets to chair the most important events."

She smiled when Sudie waggled her brows, and she continued to be amused as the housekeeper spilled out names and descriptions of the local inhabitants. There was no malice in Sudie; living in the valley allowed her to view the townspeople with a certain detachment. Eve commented on the wealth of German names.

"That's because originally this area was settled by German and Yankee farmers. Then along came the Norwegians, plus a healthy sprinkling of other Europeans before the turn of the century. Now we've got new housing developments springing up all around us like mushrooms, and we're becoming a real mixed bag."

Sudie sighed. "Like I said last night, families are scattering to the four winds. Most youngsters move on nowadays. Can't say I blame them really. Even a good-size farm won't support more than one family comfortably now. She grimaced. "So when there's no one left to take them on, farms get sold off and we get track housing."

Eve tried to think of some positive aspects. "I imagine it's unsettling to see so many changes taking place, but surely all the new housing provides opportunities for the established businesses? Not to mention a chance for entrepreneurs."

Sudie didn't seem convinced. "The established businesses, maybe. I haven't seen any sign yet, though, that the new people are going to add much to the community. Other than our tax bill for a new school, of course. You've never seen so many kids!"

"Ah, then I should have plenty of business today." The housekeeper's expression lightened at her words, and Eve asked for some paper and a pencil. "I want to make a list of things I could paint on the children's faces and, if there's time, try sketching some ideas."

Sudie brought the paper and said, "There's plenty of time. Since we're not going to church this morning, there's no rush."

"Oh, I'm sorry. I didn't realize I was keeping you."

"Not to worry. The pastor won't." The housekeeper started removing the breakfast dishes. "He's used to a light congregation in the spring. And at harvesttime."

Becoming used to her matter-of-factness, Eve decided not to worry about putting her out and went back to her list.

Adam pulled into the garage and hopped down from his truck with a spring in his step. It'd been a long time since he'd looked forward to something as much as he was today. But he didn't kid himself for a moment that his interest stemmed from anything other than his guest. The only problem he could see was that he'd get to carry Eve to and from the fairgrounds, but other than that, he probably wouldn't be able to get close to her. He'd just have to make sure she took several breaks during the day. And he'd make darn sure she took them with him.

He entered the laundry room quietly and stood studying her for a few moments. She appeared to be sketching. There was no sign of Sudie, but Sheba lay sprawled by Eve's chair.

He'd been surprised when the collie wanted to go with him in the truck at dawn, figuring she'd want to return to Eve's room after a brisk run outside. But habits are hard to break, and Sheba had been accompanying him on his morning runs since she was a puppy.

When he'd stopped at his granddad's house a while ago, Sheba disappeared. He had unlocked the kitchen door of the old farm house, telling himself it really wasn't necessary to check on things. He knew exactly how it would look. Still, he pushed the door open, wandered inside and looked around, trying to see things through Eve's eyes. A little old-fashioned, but then it would be.

He glanced at Eve as she shifted on her chair, wondering if she was an old-fashioned kind of girl. He hoped he'd have the time to find out. He found to his chagrin that her crack last night coming home still rankled. Why wasn't she even remotely interested in him? After all, it wasn't like she was involved elsewhere.

Shrugging out of his denim jacket, Adam strolled into the kitchen. "Getting a jump on your job today?"

He'd almost reached the table before Eve raised her head and, blinking, seemed to become aware of him. "Hi. I apologize if you were talking to me. I become so absorbed in what I'm doing, I tend to tune out everything around me."

"Some people would call it concentration."

"Whatever. It's what allows me to get a tremendous amount of work done." A slight frown appeared between her brows. "Except that I'm not working." She glanced down at the paper in front of her, and the pencil dangling from her fingers tilted as she clenched her fist. She seemed surprised at what she saw.

Even on the other side of the table, Adam could identify the drawing. A few bold lines delineated Sheba's body as she lay at rest on the floor, while a multitude of short strokes served as fur. "Do you mind if I take a look?"

"No, of course not." She pushed the paper across the table. "It's just a quick sketch, not very good I'm afraid."

A quick glance confirmed his first impression, then he studied the even briefer sketches Eve had made of Sheba's head higher on the paper.

"I'm not an expert, of course, but I'd have to say I can recognize my own dog." He returned the paper to the table and pointed to the drawing. "I can't tell you how many times I've seen that same expression on her face. Head on her paws, sort of looking up at me from under her lashes, like she was saying, 'Who, me?' Usually when I'm scolding her about something."

Eve laughed. "Must be a guilty conscience. When she showed up, I asked her where you were and that's the look I got."

They both looked down at the collie, who waved her plume of a tail in recognition of their attention.

If Eve had been able to catch Sheba's personality in what she called a quick sketch, what would she be able to accomplish if she took her time? Adam looked back at the table. "Would you mind if I kept this?" he asked, waving a hand at the drawing.

A quick flush tinted her pale cheeks. "No, of course not, but. . . . If I can buy a sketchbook this morning when we pick up the art supplies, I'll do a better one for you. Tonight, just in case my car's ready tomorrow."

"Thanks."

Adam didn't like his hollow feeling at hearing her speak of leaving. He'd find time for a quiet word today with Schneider to at least let him know what was wrong with Eve's car and how long it'd take to fix it. He didn't want to come home from work tomorrow night to find she'd disappeared on him.

"By the look of things, I'd say the kids are in for a treat." He motioned to the other scattered pages with discernible characters favored by kids, and his gaze flicked to her. "Didn't your father realize how talented you are?"

"It's kind of you to say so, but—"

"I'm not being kind. I'm being honest."

Seeing the same type of pain flash through her eyes that had appeared last night when Eve talked about her father, he changed the subject by looking at his watch. "We'd better round up Sudie and get a move on. Where is she?"

"I'm right here," she called from the hallway, and they heard her footsteps hit the pegged floor from the stairs.

Adam put an affectionate arm around her shoulders as she moved into the kitchen. "Been trying to improve on nature again, huh? Carl and I are going to be escorting the two prettiest women there today."

Sudie simply gave him a fond look and waved his nonsense away, but Eve felt his words warm her heart before practicality set in. She reminded herself about her earlier lecture and pushed herself slowly to her feet. Her backside felt completely numb from sitting so long.

As she stood, Adam asked, "How's the leg?"

Ruefully, Eve rubbed her bottom. "When I can feel it again, I'll let you know."

He grinned as her meaning sunk in. "I'll be right back."

He returned with a plump pillow just as her legs revived to the pins and needles stage. "This might make things more comfortable today. I'd offer to carry you, but I think you need to work the kinks out."

Even so, Adam moved up and took most of her weight on his arm when the foot of her injured leg touched down. She mumbled her thanks, charmed by his consideration even as she warned herself against it.

Sheba whined as Eve limped through the doorway and didn't seem impressed with Adam's reassurances they'd return. He steered Eve toward the garage, away from where Carl and Sudie were getting into her car, and insisted on lifting her into the truck. By the time he'd gone around and climbed in, she'd braced her foot on the dashboard. She'd also discovered her remembered reaction to his touch yesterday had been right on the money, because it'd just happened again. And Adam called Sheba fickle!

Scrambling for a distraction from her thoughts, Eve glanced over at him as he backed down the drive and started after Sudie's car. "How's the cow?"

"When I left, she was still dazed but standing."

"But she'll be all right?" At his nod, she asked out of curiosity, "What was wrong with her?"

"Low blood calcium level. That's milk fever. Common after calving."

That didn't explain a whole lot, but then there probably wasn't time for a crash course in veterinary medicine. Relieved the animal was okay, she simply said so.

"Ah, I should have known." Adam smiled over at her. "You're a real animal lover."

Her answering smile came automatically, but Eve shook her head. "I don't know, I never had a pet. And the closest I've come to other animals is in the zoo."

"You mean you never had a cat or dog growing up?" He looked astounded at the possibility when she shook her head. "Well, you may have had a deprived childhood, but you've come to the right place—and the right person—to fix that."

Eve thought about her life and decided he might just have something there. Sheba's uncomplicated affection had been wonderfully comforting last night. Not wanting to get caught up in painful memories, she squashed them back into the mental locked box where they normally resided and deliberately searched the countryside for a new distraction.

They'd already left Adam's valley and were speeding along the highway. In the distance, a herd of cows grazed in lazy contentment. They looked all of about three inches tall.

"It must feel pretty good to be able to make such a difference," Eve said.

"About what?"

"Oh, to lessen an animal's pain, make them well again. Much more satisfying than simply writing another report or developing a new budget."

"You're right, it is. Writing reports and figuring out budgets are two of my least favorite things, and I always procrastinate until the last minute." When she looked at him in surprise, Adam laughed. "I hate to disillusion you, but reports and budgets are as much a part of the small businessman as they are big business.

"I serve as veterinarian for a couple of syndicates. To get them as clients in the first place, I had to work up a plan for services and figure out what I was going to charge them. Then I have to submit a report of my activities each month with my bill." He grimaced. "As I said, not my favorite thing. In fact, I've come to dread the first of the month. There are other disadvantages as well, but we'll have to go into them later."

Eve looked up to see they'd entered the small town where they'd left her car last night. Large, two-story houses with rambling porches stood in massive, tree-shaded lots in a mixture of frame and brick. As they pulled up at a stop sign, she turned her head and glanced both ways down the narrow street to see it bisected by two others at each end. Farther down the street, a church rose from amid the cars parked around it. A bird's song carried on the light breeze; otherwise, the peace was perfect. She couldn't remember the last time she'd heard such stillness. Adam slipped the truck into gear and drove the short distance to the art supply store.

Containing all kinds of craft supplies, it turned out to be as much a surprise as Alice Rasmussen. And she, rather than being a younger version of Sudie, turned out to be vivacious and quite chic when the housekeeper introduced them. Long dark brown hair, pulled back at the sides, complemented huge, warm brown eyes.

Eve reached forward to shake hands, then realized the one Alice extended in return was bandaged.

The young woman's smile was rueful as she glanced at it. "This is taking a little getting used to. I can't tell you how much I appreciate your helping out this way. I feel unbelievably stupid for having had such an accident."

"I know the feeling," Eve admitted, "but that's why they're called accidents. After all, we wouldn't choose to injure ourselves, would we?" Bright brown eyes studied her as she leaned over and pulled up her pants leg, explaining her own accident.

Alice's rueful smile returned when she saw the puffy bruise. "Well, it's nice to meet a fellow sufferer. And doubly grateful you're willing to do this." She turned and made her way to the counter. "Now that I know about you, I can relax."

"What do you mean?" Sudie asked, trailing after them to examine the cardboard box full of supplies.

"Just that Gladys managed to twist her ankle on some loose stones at church early this morning. It's sprained. Ever since her husband called to tell me she'll be on crutches for at least a week, I've been handling Karen like eggshells, afraid I'd drop her. Since trouble comes in threes, that means Gladys is the third one, and I can relax." Her smile was wide and friendly as she beamed at Eve. "Karen's my daughter."

"Glory be!" Sudie looked worried. "What are you going to do for help with the store and Karen?"

"Good question. I thought I'd ask around at the fair today, see if I could find someone to fill in for a few weeks. Even after Gladys is off crutches, she shouldn't be standing around the store or chasing after Karen. I'll work it out. Now," she said briskly, "let's go over these supplies."

While one part of Eve's mind registered Alice's catalog of items, another worried at the woman's problem. Her first reaction had been to jump in and offer to help. But she'd kept a tight rein on her response and held her tongue. After all, she was supposed to be concentrating on herself and *her* problems. Besides, her car would probably be ready tomorrow afternoon at the latest, and she could be on her way. Somehow though, as Alice described some of the things boys had asked to have painted on their faces last year, the cabin's isolation didn't seem as inviting as it had two days ago.

Alice must have sensed her distraction because she wound up her explanation of what to expect. "Any questions?"

"Not about the face painting, but. . . . I know you are officially closed, but I wonder if I could buy a sketchpad? I promised Adam I'd do a drawing of Sheba for him, for his hospitality."

"Help yourself to whatever you need. It's the least I can do in return."

"Oh, I appreciate the offer, but it's really not necessary—"

"It is as far as I'm concerned. Here, let me show you what I've got and you choose."

Alice insisted upon giving her several charcoal pencils and a gum eraser, as well as the paper. Eve saw several things she would like to have, but decided to wait until tomorrow. Otherwise, Alice would probably try to give them to her, too. She'd stop for some art supplies before she left for the cabin. At least rediscovering her artistic ability would help to make the time pass. Sudie called to Alice with a question, and Eve continued to peruse the baskets of sale items on the counter, adding a vial of iridescent paint to her supplies for the fair.

When the men wandered over, Alice handed the box to Adam and said, "Carl, there's some things by the door. Why don't you load those?" She smiled at Eve. "Just a few amenities to make the day more bearable."

Within a few minutes, they were on their way again. As they passed the church she'd seen earlier, Eve asked, "By the way, where exactly are we going?"

"The fairgrounds. It won't take us long." Adam studied her as she studied the undulating countryside. She seemed more relaxed today. "I don't suppose you've ever seen a rodeo, have you?"

"No. Will there be one today?"

He laughed at the spark of interest in her deep blue eyes. "No, but there'll be an exhibition of riding skills at the end of the day. Pretty tame in comparison, but interesting to watch."

"Do you ride in the rodeo?"

"Not for years. I value my hide too much. Besides, I was never that good at it and it's hard to wrestle a sick cow or horse with your ribs taped."

Curious, he asked, "So what did you think of Alice?"

"She seems very happy with her life and who she is."

Adam thought about her response. Most people would have said the conventional thing, something along the lines of 'She seems like a nice person.' But Eve had spoken honestly about her feelings. From what she'd said last night, her answer mirrored her present quandary. How long had it been since something other than farming and animals raised any interest in him?

"Have you known her long?"

"Alice?" At her nod, he grinned. "Practically from the cradle. In fact, there was one point as teenagers when I suddenly developed better eyesight and a crush on her. It didn't last long though. She beat me in the barrel races that summer and my ego was too fragile then to sustain the blow."

"And so she married someone else."

"One of my best friends, as a matter of fact. I think you'll like Fisk, too."

"How about you? Have you ever been married?"

Ah, was that simple curiosity or a sign of interest? "Nope. Still footloose."

And fancy free. Or at least he had thought so until last night when a certain city girl had murmured a challenge to his ego.

Five

Adam wandered through the throng of fairgoers toward his destination, dodging racing kids, simple sightseers, and avid customers intent on their purchases. The aroma of grilled hot dogs and hamburgers that drifted on the soft breeze made his mouth water. If he'd timed things right, Eve should be ready for some lunch.

He almost groaned aloud when he saw the line of kids stretched around her at the card table he and Carl had set up. It'd doubled since he brought her some lemonade an hour ago. He shifted direction so he could see Eve under the sun umbrella Alice had provided. Three kids hung over her chair and shoulders, and another three crowded around her as she worked on Jamie McKenzie's face. But he noticed the kids were careful of Eve's leg propped up on an extra chair.

She kept up a running commentary as the outline of a bat took shape from her brush. As he closed in, he realized the boys were critiquing her work. Eve didn't seem to mind. She swished a brush in a jar of water, used it to wipe away a line, then dabbed at Jamie's face with a piece of paper towel. Dipping the brush in a pot of paint, she continued the black outline.

"Yeah, that's it," Ted Remson said, nodding approval.

The outline completed, she switched brushes and started filling in color. "So, what are you boys going to do once school's out next month?"

Jamie opened his mouth to speak, but when Eve lifted the brush he subsided with only a sigh. Ted jumped in with, "The very first thing we're going to do is go fishin'." Adam smiled as he remembered teaching the boys. "Dr. Wagner's got a great fishin' hole, and he lets us use the rowboat. When we get too hot, we go swimmin'.' "

"I'm going fishin' too." Jamie's younger sister looked at Eve worshipfully from the side of her chair.

Melissa's nine-year-old face quickly became clouded, however, when Jamie pulled back from Eve's fingers holding him in place and said, "No, you're not."

"Am, too! Momma said I'm old enough to go with you this summer."

Before Jamie could respond, Eve lowered the brush and arched her brows. He subsided without a word, satisfying himself with a scowl at his sister. Rinsing her brush, Eve said, "You go all the way to Dr. Wagner's valley to go fishing?"

"We live just on the other side," Melissa told her.

"It's not that far," Ted added, " 'cause we can get there on a bike trail from town."

Eve changed colors on her brush. "I thought maybe you rode your horses there."

"Don't have a horse," Ted informed her. "Sometimes Dr. Wagner gives us rides on his."

"That's nice of him."

"Yeah, he's a pretty nice guy. He's awfully strict about taking care of pets though." Adam bit his lip at Ted's pronouncement.

"Do you all have pets?"

She was bombarded with names and descriptions of sundry animals. Before Adam realized what was happening, Jamie rose from his chair and Melissa slipped into it. Without missing a beat, Eve rinsed her brush and started the outline of a butterfly while the litany of pets went on. Two more kids joined the line.

He edged his way into the group, relieved to see paint already on the faces clustered around Eve. "Hi, guys. Hey, nice designs." When he'd examined and commented on one, he said, "What do you think the chances are of Miss Sutton being able to have some lunch?"

He heard no audible groans, but they were clearly unhappy. Adam said, "As much as Miss Sutton enjoys painting your faces, she needs to take a break now and then." Pulling on Suzy Jefferson's pigtails, he added, "You don't want her to be so weak she can't lift her paintbrush, do you?" Suzie, the next in line, wagged her head solemnly, but some of the others giggled.

Eve rinsed her brush and said, "You'll be my first customer when I return at . . ." She looked at her watch.

"In one hour," Adam said before she could name a time. "Tell your mother you need to be back at one-thirty, okay?"

"I'm second," Suzy's sister said.

A chorus of voices called out. "Not a bad idea," he agreed. "Count off and remember your number. If anyone gets delayed, the next one can go ahead. When you show up, you can have a turn. Understand?"

He turned from their retreating backs to Eve's amused blue eyes as she cleaned paint from her hands. "You handle kids very well."

"I had a great teacher. My granddad never talked down to me." He offered his hand to pull her up and gave her a few moments to regain the circulation in her legs. "I noticed you didn't do a bad job of corralling them yourself." In fact, she'd looked very natural with a gang of kids around her.

Replacing the lids on jars of paint, she wrinkled her brow. "I think maybe it was because I was interested in them. I listened to what they had to say."

"You mean your technique didn't come from years of practice on friends' children?" When she shook her head, he grinned and said, "Deprived adulthood, too. That's okay. You don't have to worry because you're a natural." He placed his hand under her left elbow and steered her toward the food tent.

Their progress kept being interrupted by friends who stopped Adam to chat. He realized the attraction was the lovely lady on his arm after the fourth interruption and the flow of questions directed toward her.

He realized word had spread when he saw his office dragon bearing down on them. "Hi, Martha. Have you eaten yet?"

"Yes, I have. Why?"

"Because we only have fifty minutes before Eve has to be back to paint more little faces, and she needs to get off a sore leg. So if you want to interrogate her, you'll have to join us."

"Interrogate, indeed!" The older woman frowned at Adam, but turned a concerned gray gaze on Eve and moved to support her on the other side. "You poor dear. Did one of those hooligans run into you?"

"No, I'm afraid I have to assume full responsibility."

Before his secretary-receptionist-assistant animal holder could charge in with more questions, he said, "Eve is a guest of mine." He lowered Eve to a bench and threw an arm around Martha's shoulders. "Martha Diehl, my right arm. She runs the clinic . . . and me."

"Only when you let me," she answered saucily and sat down opposite Eve.

Knowing when he was beaten, Adam asked Eve what she wanted to eat, told Martha he would buy her a drink, and left her to it. He figured she'd have Eve's life story out of her, chapter and verse, within ten minutes.

Somehow he wasn't too surprised when he returned with the food and found their table full of his friends. Eve scooted over to make room for him next to her. Looking around as he sat down, he said, "Didn't know I was so popular." He slid a winking glance at Eve as he added, "Or are you trying to horn in on my territory?"

A blush warmed her cheeks as Jim Hummel asked Adam when he'd first noticed signs of delusion. "Myself, I never needed any help finding a pretty woman. Witness my beautiful wife here."

Connie withdrew her hand after her husband had planted several kisses along its back and, with a laugh, turned to Eve. "The only way to handle them when they act like five-year-olds is to ignore them." Even so, she leaned over and kissed the side of Jim's neck.

Her gaze was bright and interested as she asked, "Have you had a chance to look around yet or have the little monsters kept you too busy?" At Martha's frown and the *tsking* sound the older woman made, she added, "I can say that because one of the little monsters is mine."

Eve smiled back. "They've kept me busy. We passed some beautiful quilts on our way here. Maybe I'll have a chance to stop on my way back."

On the other side of her, Clarel Krpan asked, "Was there anything in particular? We could pick it up for you since you're probably going to be inundated with kids after lunch. I saw the beautiful butterfly you did for Melissa McKenzie. Those iridescent colors are gorgeous."

"Thanks."

The praise pleased Eve, who had felt rejuvenated this morning at the simple task of painting faces. Hesitant at first, her brush began to move more quickly as she gained confidence in her ability to satisfy the children's demands. It felt wonderfully liberating to be doing something simply for the pleasure of it.

When she realized Clarel was still smiling at her, Eve remembered her question. "Thanks for the offer, but there's nothing I really need. I don't even need the quilt, but it looked lovely."

From beside his wife, Dan Krpan said dryly, "We don't need half the things we picked up this morning, either. But as Clarel keeps reminding me, it's for a worthy cause."

The talk turned to the different things everyone had found. Listening to them, Eve decided Sudie was a pretty good judge of character. The only surprise had been the ages of the various couples, most of them contemporaries of Adam.

They were rising when Alice stopped by the table with Karen, who promptly held her arms out to Adam. Alice complimented Eve on the great job she'd done while Eve kept a distracted eye on the baby. Somehow it didn't look incongruous for the strapping six footer to be bouncing a tiny toddler on his arm.

When a man who could only have been Alice's husband came up and put his arm around her, Eve realized all the couples shared an easy intimacy they weren't afraid to exhibit in public. And she'd always been afraid of any intimacy.

Gazing at the couples around her, she thought she'd never met so many open and friendly people. She couldn't help but wonder if their response would be the same if they knew who she really was; she knew Adam's reaction would be different.

Acknowledging the introduction to Fisk Rasmussen, she turned to go back to her face painting when Martha asked Alice if she'd found anyone to fill in for the injured Gladys.

"Not yet. But you can help by passing the word for me."

Eve hesitated a moment, the unbroken quiet of the cabin shimmering in her memory. Then this morning's activities superimposed themselves, and she knew she'd be bored out of her mind within a week by herself. "Alice, I'm not sure I fit what you're looking for, but I'd like to volunteer."

She knew she'd done the right thing when relief swept over the young woman's face. "You're a lifesaver. Honestly, Karen's no trouble. She takes a nap right after lunch, so she's only awake about an hour before I return."

Eve felt a sinking sensation in the bottom of her stomach. She'd forgotten that Gladys watched the baby as well as the store. Oh well, how difficult could it be? Her MBA certainly guaranteed she was smart enough to learn to diaper a baby and, if teenagers could babysit, so could she. "No problem."

Alice leaned forward and engulfed her in a quick hug. "Thanks. That's a load off my mind. I'll stop by at the end of the day to collect the painting things so you and Adam don't have to bother with them any further. I'll talk to you then about the timing."

Handing Karen to her father, Adam beamed a look of approval at Eve. Her last doubts evaporated with his warm smile. He glanced down at his watch and said, "Oops, we're running late. Sorry, folks, but there's going to be a line of kids waiting for Eve."

The other couples strolled along with them. Connie said, "I'm glad you're staying, Eve. I'll drop in tomorrow and say hello."

"Me, too," Clarel added. "Look, there're the quilts. Why don't you point out which one you're interested in and I'll bring it over. I'm sure the girls won't mind."

Eve returned to work enveloped in a warm glow, which grew as the afternoon wore on and people dropped by to introduce themselves. One of those was Roy Schneider, who told her he'd look at her car first thing in the morning and let her know what he found. More surprising was the fact that several of Adam's friends dropped by to bring her a cold drink and chat for a few minutes.

The only discordant note occurred late in the afternoon when Eve felt someone watching her. Which was strange, because people had been staring at her all day. This time she sensed disapproval and raised her gaze from a half-finished figure to see a slim, dark-haired young woman frowning at her from the edge of the crowd. She couldn't remember being introduced to her. If nothing else, she would have remembered the woman's clothes since they shouted money.

Definitely unfriendly vibes there. Nonplussed, Eve smiled tentatively. An outright glare rewarded her friendly overture before the young woman turned and disappeared into the milling crowd.

The little girl whose face she was working on moved restlessly and, shrugging, Eve forgot all about the mysterious young woman.

When she was released from her painting duties, Adam took Eve on a tour of the 4-H fair. He wanted to carry her, but she demurred, saying she needed the exercise.

Surprised to see a flash of disappointment in his eyes, she realized his medical concern had edged over into the personal. She couldn't help the spurt of satisfaction accompanying that thought. Nor could she ignore the pleasure she felt at grasping the solid support of his muscular forearm when he insisted she lean on him.

"Doctor's orders," he said.

"Ah, but I'm not one of your patients. I've only two legs."

"Don't think I haven't noticed. Makes a nice change of pace for me."

Still smiling a moment later when long, low buildings came into view, he said, "Let me show you some satisfied customers."

Animal cries carried over the hum of milling people's voices as they strolled down an aisle between stalls on either side. Eve cooed over the darling lambs and the piglets' tiny corkscrew tails amid straw and sawdust.

They entered the next building where Adam said some of his former patients were housed. Eve took one look at the huge animal in the first stall and stepped back a pace when it put its head over the low door at their approach.

"That's a cow?"

He looked at her strangely. "Why, what's wrong?"

"That thing's big enough to put a saddle on!"

He laughed, but she remembered the cows she'd seen from a distance earlier. Obviously propinquity made a difference.

"If you think these ladies are big, wait till you see the bulls." He ran a big hand over the cow's head, patting her affectionately. "Come on, she won't hurt you."

When the animal turned her head toward Adam and practically nuzzled him, Eve patted the side of its sleek neck. The cow edged closer to Adam, burrowing under his arm, and she smiled at the effect he seemed to have on the female of any species.

Hadn't she herself lapped up his attention last night and today? Adam's consideration of her comfort and his regard for her feelings had gone a long way to soothe her ego after Richard's betrayal.

Under his tutelage, Eve gained confidence in approaching the animals and discovered she actually enjoyed it. There was something about the big, peaceful cows and their acceptance that touched her.

When she tried to put it into words, Adam smiled. "These animals have been treated well and trust humans. They have no reason not to. Unless they're mistreated by someone, they'll respond like an overgrown puppy and eat up any attention you show them."

"Pretty much like people," she said without thinking.

"Yes." He put his arm around her shoulder and led her toward the exit. "But just between you and me, I've found that animals are more honest than people."

Once more Eve felt a touch of guilt at being there under false pretenses. Then with a shake of her head, she decided it was wasted emotional energy: no one would ever know since she'd be there such a short time.

They left the hay-scented stalls behind and made their way toward the riding ring. Thinking back over the day, Eve realized Adam had bolstered her confidence in several areas—not the least of which was her ability to attract a friend as nice as Adam Wagner.

Two hours later, he ushered her into the local watering hole for dinner. The first person Eve saw upon entering was the mysterious woman from earlier in the day. She couldn't imagine what she'd done to antagonize the young lady, who frowned at her entrance, but decided not to worry about it as a waitress led them to a table on the opposite side of the room.

After placing an order, they satisfied their thirst with long draughts of the beer Adam had ordered. The day had turned as warm as Sudie had predicted.

"So," Adam said, rubbing a thumb over his mustache, "why didn't you practice child psychology on your friends' offspring?"

She had noticed that the Wisconsin inhabitants didn't hesitate to ask what was on their minds and smiled. Then, remembering nannies and au pairs, she shrugged helplessly. "I was around them, but. . . ."

Taking a deep breath, Eve avoided that landmine and really thought about those long ago times. Finally, picking at the label on her beer bottle, she said, "I think in retrospect it was because my energies were elsewhere. I started working the summer I graduated from college, and it wasn't long before my father started trying to convince me I needed to go to graduate school."

A quick glance showed Adam looked interested, so she continued. "I held out against him for a year, but eventually I did what he wanted, as I usually did. I kept in touch with my friends, of course, but by then my focus was on studying to produce good grades while they produced babies. I found it harder to keep up the relationships. We kept drifting apart as our lives took different paths. After grad school, I plunged into work again and somehow never picked up the threads of my old life."

"And you never married."

Shuddering, Eve could feel the heat stealing up her throat. "Uh, no." Surprising herself, she said, "Again in retrospect, I think it was because I made my father and pleasing him the focus of my energies. That didn't leave much time for matchmaking by my, by then, few real friends." She'd even just about given up on her old daydreams when her father had died.

Tired of psychoanalyzing herself—or afraid to probe more deeply into tender territory—she switched the tables. "What about you? How come you never married?"

"All those acres to be reclaimed, remember? Somehow, my granddad's dream became mine and it became a habit to think only of them." A roll of his broad shoulders said it didn't bother him. "And since no one interesting turned up to distract me, I find myself teaching other people's children how to fish and ride." His smile was self-deprecating as he tilted the beer bottle to his mouth.

"Yeah, I heard about that earlier." Her grin faded as her curiosity increased. "How do you find time to do everything? The farm, your veterinary duties, your business, the children?"

"Oh, I don't know. The most important thing at the moment sort of pushes everything else to the background. Somehow it all gets done."

Eve wasn't deceived by his casual tone. Adam Wagner was a more complicated man than appeared on the surface, and a more caring one. Then she remembered his stopping to help her, and she realized she shouldn't have been surprised at the time he took to teach Ted and Jamie how to hold a fishing pole or how to ride properly. She warmed toward him at the realization he was more intent on helping others get what they wanted rather than the other way around.

They took turns exploring their youth, tall tales of their exploits on the lake, and probing gently at the hidden crevices of their lives. With the noise level rising around them, Eve found herself leaning more and more across the table to hear Adam. So engrossed were they that it took several moments to realize Fisk was standing at their table with a bemused smile.

"I've been deputized to ask you to join us for a drink," he said, waving a hand at their table, "since you've finished your dinner."

Eve glanced down at the table in surprise. She hardly remembered eating, but the remains of their pizza sat in mute testimony that they had. She'd never been so drawn to anyone, so taken out of herself that she forgot who she was and what she was doing or why. Adam Wagner was having the strangest effect on her. By mutual agreement, they rose to move to the tables pushed together by his friends.

Eve noticed the strange young woman again and that her antics seemed to increase in volume as Adam neared their table. He, though, was completely unaware of her as he introduced Eve to those of his friends she didn't know. Finally, finding herself next to Alice, she leaned closer and asked who the woman was.

Alice flicked an irritated glance at the noisy crew. "Oh, dear. Jane's being her usual lovely self again. Jane Hartwig," she clarified for Eve.

The group had attracted frowns and the attention of just about everyone in the combination tavern and pizza restaurant. Suddenly, Jane Hartwig rose and announced she was bored. She leaned into her companion and ran her fingers up his shoulder, but Eve caught the glance Jane slanted toward them from under lowered lids. Adam was oblivious to her performance as he talked to one of his friends.

The waitress approached to take their beer order and, the next time Eve looked up, the younger crowd had disappeared.

* * *

Though the day had been sunny and warm, the night air had a decided nip to it as the group said its good nights outside several hours later.

The coolness reached Eve, even enveloped as she was in a slight beer buzz. She wasn't a tee-totaler, but usually she never had more than one cocktail since most of the social functions she attended were business related. She'd had no such responsibility this evening and, caught up in the varied discussions swirling around her, she'd paid no attention when her glass had been topped off repeatedly. She'd simply enjoyed being a part of the lively men and women surrounding her.

"I like your friends," she told Adam after he'd helped her into the truck and climbed in himself.

He chuckled in the semi-darkness before starting the engine. "I think it's evident they like you, too."

Still feeling somewhat guilty over her deception, she said, "What is it about this town? I've never met so many nice and accommodating people in one place as I did today."

"Brighton's like every other place. Most of the people are nice, but there are a few who could use a course in good manners." Adam pulled out onto the highway behind several of his friends' cars. "In all honesty, you're responsible for a good deal of what happened today."

"Me?" Eve sat up a little straighter and blinked eyelids that had begun to feel heavy.

"Most were responding to your goodwill gesture of helping Alice. She's very popular. Born and raised in this area, she's accumulated a lot of friends over the years. Then, when they discovered you were staying and helping out at the store as well, you won over even the hardest hearts." He flashed her a grin from under that sexy mustache, and Eve found herself smiling back at him. "Of course, it doesn't hurt that you're the friendly sort yourself."

"I've been called a lot of things in my life, but I can't remember hearing that one before."

"Stick with us, and we'll make a believer out of you, City Girl."

When Adam had first called her that—what, only a little more than twenty-four hours ago—his voice had contained a teasing quality. Now Eve thought she detected a fond undertone, and a fuzzy warning bell tried to make itself heard before the remembered warmth of her reception and acceptance by Alice and the others distracted her. After all, this was what she wanted, wasn't it? For people to take her as she was and not the persona from the mold she'd forced herself into to please her father? Damned straight. And she liked the freedom of going with her instincts. So far it'd been very rewarding.

Adam pulled the truck up to a four-way stop and looked over at her. "If I haven't said it before, I'm glad you're staying. I think you'll do better here among friends than you would by yourself somewhere."

He eased forward and added, "Even though my granddad's house is only a short distance from mine, you don't have to worry about constant company. You can see as much or as little of Sudie, Carl, and I as you want." He chuckled to himself. "I'd better remember to say something to Sudie about that just to make sure."

"What's your grandfather's house like?"

"Just an old, two-story farmhouse. Don't worry. You have all the amenities. In fact, there's a bedroom and bath on the first floor, so the second floor can stay closed off. Plus there's bedding and dishes. Everything's under dust sheets now, but Sudie airs and cleans it a little every three months so it's in pretty good shape. I'll have Martha call for the electric and phone to be connected tomorrow for you."

"I appreciate your offer to use it gratis, but I'd feel more comfortable if I paid you something."

If he had his way, she'd stay in his house and let him take care of her. From their earlier conversation, it sounded as if no one ever had. But he acknowledged he couldn't ask Sudie to stay on as chaperone—not that he wanted one—and he knew without thinking about it that Eve wouldn't stay under his roof without her.

"Uh-uh," Adam said, prepared to argue with her. "Conditions already laid down and accepted. No changing horses in mid-stream."

He looked over as she tilted her head toward him with the backwash of the headlights playing along a determined jawline. He sensed her strong will and didn't want it turned against him. "Tell you what. If it'll make you feel any better, you pay the phone and electric bills. And once in awhile, you can throw in a home cooked meal for me." He'd mentioned the meal at the last moment, but realized it'd been a stroke of genius. At least he'd made sure he'd see her once in awhile. "Is it a deal?" he asked, turning to see her reaction.

"I thought you said Sudie cooked for you." He couldn't read her expression clearly, but her voice sounded doubtful.

"I said that Sudie usually leaves something for me to warm up for dinner. Depending upon what it is and what time I eat it, it's either okay or like eating shoe leather. It'd be nice to have a normal hot meal once in awhile."

"I'm not the world's greatest cook—" She broke off with a laugh as he pulled into the driveway. "Who am I kidding? I'm probably one of the worst, but I could try. It's the least I can do since you're providing a roof over my head."

Adam went around to the passenger side and, because he knew he wouldn't be able to use her injury as an excuse to hold her after today, he scooped Eve up in his arms. He inhaled the tantalizing scent that had teased him all day, light and fresh like the woman he held, but with a seductive note that stirred his desire. He felt a great deal of satisfaction when she settled against him with a little sigh. Out of the corner of his eye, the overhead light gleamed on the polished exterior of his rarely used sedan, his stepmother's car which had been kept in excellent condition.

"By the way, if Schneider says your car is going to be out of action, don't worry about wheels. You can use this one."

Her muffled "Thanks" came from where her head rested on her arm across his shoulder.

When he reached the back door, Adam paused for Eve to open it, but she remained snuggled in his arms without moving. He looked down to see her eyes closed. Poor baby. They'd worn her out today. He dipped his knees and managed to open the storm door a crack. Wedging his boot into it, he widened the gap and struggled to get a grip on the doorknob without bumping Eve's leg. A bark from Sheba welcomed him on the other side.

"Hush, girl," he warned just as Eve stirred against him.

"Sorry," she mumbled, reaching forward to help.

Sheba danced around them, woofing in excitement. Adam set Eve down in the kitchen lit with the light over the stove where a note lay propped against the tea kettle. Pulling out a chair for her, he said, "You'd better say hello or she'll keep it up till she wakes Sudie."

He breathed a little easier when Eve subsided onto the chair and bent over Sheba. But his arms still felt her thistle-light weight and, even worse, he remembered the feel of her. The dim light surrounding them only increased the aura of intimacy, and Adam wished it were for real. But he had to give her a chance to regain her equilibrium from a broken engagement. He didn't want to be accused of taking advantage of a woman on the rebound.

Hearing her yawn, he said, "Bedtime."

As if it were the most natural thing in the world, she held up her arms and linked them around his neck as he lifted her. The trip upstairs became sheer torture with her forehead resting against his neck and her scent filling his senses. He pulled her tighter against him, but managed to keep his hands still by reminding himself she was a guest in his home.

The ridiculously small lamp on the dresser cast an intimate glow in her room as he lowered Eve to the bed with its pulled-down covers. His hands slid away slowly and came to rest on the mattress on either side of her as she faced him. The need to discover what she tasted like speared through him, to be met with an equally strong desire to put his stamp on her. Surely it wouldn't hurt to take just one tiny taste . . . if he was very careful and moved very slowly so as not to frighten her.

Eve looked up at him, her eyes heavy lidded, and he wished it could have been from passion—something he'd not felt for a very long time. He slowly raised one hand until it cupped her chin.

"Sleep well, little one."

Moving just as slowly, he lowered his mouth until it covered hers in a gentle kiss. Their lips clung together as he pulled back.

"Sleep well," he repeated in a whisper and left while he could.

Six

The next morning Eve didn't know who was more excited, Sudie, Adam or herself, as they ushered her through the back door of his grandfather's house.

She took several steps forward and turned three hundred and

sixty degrees in the mid-morning sunshine that flooded the room, staring in amazement. A fieldstone fireplace dominated one end of the huge area, the equivalent of a family room and kitchen combined. Highly polished oak floors gleamed with reflected light, which also cast a warm glow on the blue and gold plaid furniture arranged around the fireplace. A long, rectangular table with eight chairs split the room. Once again her expectations had been confounded. "It's lovely."

Adam's smile grew. "I talked granddad into renovating it about ten years ago. The downstairs, that is, which is all he'd allow. As long as he insisted on living here, I wanted him to be comfortable." His fingers trailed over the gleaming surface of the old oak dining table, and she realized many of his memories were bound up in this room, this house.

"Good heavens, Sudie," Eve said, looking at the pristine countertops. "Didn't you leave anything for me to do?"

"All I did was give it a lick and a promise and aired the sheets for you. It didn't need much more because I gave it a thorough cleaning about a month ago. The bedroom's back here with an adjoining bath."

That room, too, had been enlarged. Adam pointed at the wainscoting on one wall. "Part of the original living room. The old bedroom was made into an office for my granddad. It's empty now. I thought you might use it for painting. Let me show you."

Sudie trailed after them, and Eve gave a silent sigh of thanks. She didn't know if she was ready yet to handle a one-on-one conversation with Adam.

Like the bedroom, one end of the room was a wall of glass windows overlooking a slightly different aspect of the valley. "It's perfect."

He shrugged. "It's a little old-fashioned and the appliances are practically antiques. And the upstairs is a warren of small, cramped rooms. Granddad," he said, shrugging again.

They'd wandered back to the main room where Eve said, "I think he must have been very happy here. I know I will be, too."

Adam showed her how to adjust the thermostat and turn on the stove. Though she'd been restrained around him this morning, she turned toward him now with a big smile. "It was kind of you to take the time to show me around."

"Oh well, you know what I think about kind. I wanted to be here." His gaze was warm as it touched hers, causing her pulse to accelerate. "But I've got some more calls to make. I'd better hit the road again if I want to make my clinic before noon. I'll give you a lift to Schneider's later if your car is ready. Otherwise, I'll . . . see you around."

Eve felt loneliness closing in as Sudie and Adam prepared to leave, but she ruthlessly strangled the sensation. It wasn't like they were leaving her alone forever; she'd probably see them every day. She followed them out the door, reminding herself how much lonelier it would have been at the cabin and that this was what she needed, to learn to be by herself without Tilly or Sudie around to take care of things for her. Besides, after last night, things were getting a little complicated and she needed the time to think.

Adam started down the flagstone path, then stopped. "The barn," he said, nodding toward the weathered building at the end of the lane between the two houses. "I completely forgot. I don't have time now, but I'll show you around this evening so you can go riding whenever you want." Waving, he started toward his house.

"You need anything, just give me a call," Sudie said. "Or walk down. If I don't hear from you, I'll come myself in a day or so."

Sheba paced after her and Adam for a few steps, then turned back as if to see what was keeping Eve. When she moved back toward the house, the collie whined, turning her head between Eve and the others. She barked sharply and sat, clearly confused about who to follow.

Halfway to his driveway, Adam shouted, "Sheba, stay!" The dog looked over her shoulder at Eve, then got up and padded toward her. Adam called out, "Just bring her to the house with you when you leave for the store." With a wave, he turned away.

Eve ruffled the dog's fur, glad of her company. "Just let me get my few things settled, girl, then we'll go for a walk." Excitement had risen again at the prospect of her fresh start, and she was anxious to explore her new home and surroundings.

"There, I think that's it."

Eve looked down at the disposable diaper she'd just put on

Karen. Maybe it didn't fit as snug as the wet one she'd removed, but it'd do. Before she could redo the romper snaps, the baby twisted her little body as she reached for a toy, and the tabs holding the diaper in place promptly popped open. Eve pressed them closed, but as soon as she let go, they peeled back again.

"Great! What happened to the stick'um?" She released a big sigh, which made Karen wave her arms. "I don't know, sweetie. It looked so easy when your mother did it."

Gathering Karen's little feet between the fingers of one hand like she'd seen Alice do, she removed the useless diaper and noticed a blob of petroleum jelly. She looked at her fingers: they were slick from the jelly she'd applied to Karen's bottom to help ward off diaper rash.

Reaching into the box for a wet wipe to clean her hands, she told the baby, "See, I told you I could learn to do it. As Adam says, 'Stick with me, kid.' "

Successful at last, Eve looked at her watch. "Well, that only took twenty minutes." She tickled the baby's stomach and grinned. "It's all gravy from here."

She heated Karen's formula and settled to feed her when the bell over the door announced an arrival. Juggling the baby and her bottle, she stepped into the front of the store. Two young women stood before the wall of paintings for sale that Alice had explained contained work on consignment.

"If I can be of any help, let me know," Eve said from beside the counter.

The women turned slightly at the sound of her voice, and she stiffened. Jane Hartwig, dressed in a linen suit and heels, stared back at her coolly before turning back to the paintings. It was almost as if the young woman had carried the battle to Eve. She became sure of it when Jane's comments carried back to her.

"No, too dreary." Jane's friend indicated another painting. "Too pedestrian. There's absolutely nothing of value to be found here." Jane turned her head and stared, her gaze traveling down Eve's figure from her casual shirt and blue jeans to her sneakers. "Nothing of value at all."

Eve seethed, but kept a calm expression on her face. Not by so much as a twitch would she let the little witch know she'd understood the challenge, and the slur, aimed at her. "I'm so sorry you ladies didn't find anything to interest you," she said pleasantly. "Do try us again."

Deliberately, she disappeared into the back room. No game was much fun if your opponent refused to play. But the effort cost her and, when she sank into the rocking chair, she realized her knees were shaking. But then came the sound of the front door slamming on its hinges, and the ghost of a smile appeared.

Eve looked down at the baby watching her with huge eyes and started to rock back and forth. She told Karen solemnly, "If little girls want to play with fire, then they have to carry something more than ineffectual matches made of spite."

There was no denying the satisfaction she felt at coming out on top in the little skirmish, but the ramifications worried Eve. Whether Adam knew it or not, Jane had obviously set her sights on him and was determined enough to try and scare off her competition.

Some competition. She hadn't even known she was in the game until last night. But she should have, Eve acknowledged. She'd felt a connection with Adam from the first; she'd just hid from it. What kind of person did that make her, to break off an engagement one day and be attracted to someone else practically the next?

Probably all too human. She smiled at the twists of fate that had led to her present predicament. Or to her present position of power. It all depended upon how one looked at it. She might be attracted to Adam, but there was no way she was going to act on it. Except Jane Hartwig didn't know that.

She had enough of an agenda just trying to decide what to do about being the owner of an electronics business she now knew she didn't want to run. Exactly what she *did* want to do was another question, the second on her list. Following a distant third was what to do about the immature Miss Hartwig.

If there was some way to protect her friend Adam and at the same time trip up Jane Hartwig, then she'd do it. Still, that didn't mean she'd fall in with the plan he seemed to have in mind. But because she *was* human, Eve was tempted after his kiss last night.

She sighed as she remembered feeling more of a physical response from that light brush of lips than she had in several months of Richard trying to put the make on her. Unfortunately, that reminded her of Richard's parting taunt that she was a cold fish and responsible for his looking elsewhere. She was glad now she'd held out against his pleas to consummate their relationship during their two-month engagement.

It wasn't that she'd planned it that way. Richard had been so sweet and patient with her that she'd been willing to risk another try at happiness. After all, it'd been almost ten years since first being disastrously smitten with love. Unfortunately, Richard hadn't continued to be patient once they were officially engaged. She'd been nervous she wouldn't measure up and hadn't been able to relax. At first, he'd teased her. Then his teasing turned to cajoling, which only increased her anxiety. Eventually his growing frustration only reinforced her inability to respond, and she reached the point where she even dreaded physical contact during a kiss.

It was strange then that she'd felt such an immediate affinity with Adam. And when he'd kissed her last night, she'd been so caught up in the moment that her mind hadn't played its usual game of twenty questions: should her lips be open or closed, should she put her arms around him, what if he wanted more than just a kiss? In fact, she'd enjoyed it so much she'd been disappointed when he drew back. Why this reaction with Adam when twice before she'd felt nothing more than pleasant curiosity? Maybe if Adam had been her first love. . . .

Then her practicality reasserted itself. Who was she kidding? Adam might be making interested moves on Eve Sutton, the woman whose second-hand car had broken down, but there was no guarantee he'd look twice at Eve Sutton, proprietor of World-wide Electronics. He just didn't happen to know they were one and the same. But once he did, Eve had a feeling she'd be lumped in the same bracket with the spoiled Jane Hartwig. And that hurt.

Eve pushed her heavily laden shopping cart down yet another grocery store aisle. She'd been at this for over an hour and she still wasn't through. She sighed. Time consumption wasn't the only thing she hadn't known about grocery shopping; she also hadn't realized how complicated it was. The few items she'd picked up in years past while at the cabin hadn't qualified her for this. She began to regret her rash promise to fix a few meals for Adam.

After handling Karen successfully this afternoon, not to mention her confrontation with Jane, Eve considered herself on a roll. It'd been a long time since home economic classes in high school; in college she'd lived in the sorority house where meals were provided; at home, Tilly cooked for her on the rare occasions she didn't eat out somewhere. So what if she didn't know how to cook? How much could there be to it?

She'd bought herself a cookbook that afternoon and studied it in the parking lot, trying to get an idea of the supplies she'd need. Only to be confronted in the grocery store with confusing varieties: did she want all-purpose flour, self-rising flour, the bleached or non-bleached kind? And when she wasn't confronted with variations on the same product, she still had multiple labels to contend with. All these choices were driving her crazy.

"Hi, Eve." She looked up to see Alice bearing down on her. "Goodness, it looks like you're shopping for an army."

"The pantry was bare, so I'm starting from ground zero." She looked at the mountain of food and cleaning products in her cart. "Though by the time I get this home and put it all away, I'm going to be starved. Maybe I'll pick up a microwave dinner for this evening so I won't have to worry about it."

"Good idea. Before you go. . . ."

Thirty minutes later, Eve had agreed to meet Connie, Clarel and Alice for lunch the next day, finished her shopping and pulled out of the parking lot. Dusk settled as she drove, and she worried about being able to find her landmarks. At least Adam's car was proving more dependable than hers. Mr. Schneider had reported her fuel filter was damaged. He'd have to order one and it would be a couple of days before it arrived. Once more she was in Adam's debt, since she'd need his car to get back and forth to the art store. She'd better study her new cookbook tonight and get started on repaying him.

Full dark had descended before she turned onto the summit road, and lights blazed at Adam's as she passed. He was probably eating his dinner. She was so hungry she'd settle for *anything* at this point, no matter how overdone or dried out it was. At least she had electricity when she finally found the light switch.

By the time she toted the last bag of groceries inside, Eve had a splitting headache and the wound on her leg throbbed. She'd also broken a fingernail, had a bag split open and dump its contents on the ground, and she was tired. Not to mention hungry. Whatever she was paying Tilly, it wasn't enough!

Deciding if she ever sat down she wouldn't be able to get up again, she started digging through the bags to find her microwave dinner. At this point, it would only serve as an appetizer, but she had plenty of things to add to the menu . . . if she could figure out how to fix them fast enough.

"At last!" She held up the softening carton like a prize and shoved aside cans and boxes and bags of groceries on the counter looking for the microwave. Where *was* the silly thing? In desperation, she put all of the still-full bags on the floor. Her stomach growled as she faced the fact there was no microwave. She turned the carton over and read the directions for a conventional oven. Forty minutes at four hundred degrees. The only thing left to do was scream. "Arghhhhhh!" Which didn't help, but it certainly made her feel better.

Adam knocked on the back door to his granddad's house for the second time in two hours. The first time Eve hadn't been home and, almost dusk, he'd become concerned. He saw her drive by later since he'd been watching for her and headed for the door, only to stop as he pulled it open. He'd promised her she'd have privacy and here he was racing off to check on her like she was sixteen instead of—whatever she was.

Sheba woofed at him as he stood there with the doorknob still in his hand. "Yeah, I know, girl. I want to see her, too, but I think we'd better wait awhile."

He'd told her this morning that he'd come over this evening to take her around the barn. Maybe this was her polite way of letting him know he'd overstepped the boundaries last night.

Hell, he'd known he was rushing his fences, but the agony of not knowing what she tasted like couldn't be borne any longer. And it had been every bit as good as he'd imagined; better even.

Adam paced the floor until he figured he'd given her time enough. He shot out the door, only to retrace his steps when he realized he'd forgotten the apple pie Sudie had baked for Eve.

He held it in front of him now like a peace offering when she appeared in the doorway. "Welcome to the neighborhood. Sudie baked it for you."

"Oh, food! How wonderful." She'd taken it from him and half turned away before she said, "Come in. I found the coffee pot and made some coffee. We could have some with the pie."

As she greeted Sheba, Adam stepped in and came to a halt at the sight before him. Cans and boxes stood in orderly rows on the countertop, as well as in lines on the floor. An empty aluminum foil tray sat on the table, an apple core resting in its center, mute testimony to the type of dinner she'd eaten. He wished he'd followed his first instinct to charge over here when he first saw her car lights so she could have shared his casserole.

Retrieving cups and saucers from the cupboard, she saw him looking at the groceries. "At first I began shoving them in anywhere until I realized I'd never be able to find anything. So I started over with a more methodical approach. Since I've changed my mind twice about where to put things, it seemed easier to organize it all first before putting any of it away."

He'd noticed the lines of cans separated by vegetables, fruits and soup. Then he blinked. This was one for the books: she even had them alphabetized individually. "You certainly seem to have organization down pat."

She waved him toward the table. "Tilly always says if a job's worth doing, it's worth doing well."

"Tilly?"

"She's like a mother to me." Eve sat and immediately dug into the pie while Sheba flopped at her feet. "Ummm. You have no idea how good this tastes."

"Sudie's a good cook. I didn't mean to imply last night that she wasn't. It's just that by the time I get to eat whatever it is she's fixed, it's past its prime, so to speak."

Eve had already eaten half her piece of pie and he had yet to take his first bite. He'd just cut into it when he heard a choking noise and looked up to see her setting down her coffee cup, sputtering and coughing. "Are you okay?"

Nodding, she made a face. "Oh, that's awful!" He reached for his cup, but Eve stopped him. "No, believe me, you don't want to try it." She rose and collected their cups. "I don't know what I did wrong. Of course, the coffee pot is different than I'm used to, but still—Ugh!" She shivered and poured the coffee down the drain.

Adam glanced toward the stove where his granddad's faithful old aluminum coffee pot sat on the burner. "Over the years I must have given granddad three different kinds of coffee makers. He always went back to that one," he said, waving toward the stove. "I could never figure out how long you were supposed to boil the coffee in that aluminum thing."

"Obviously I can't either." Eve sat back down and finished her pie in two bites. "That's so good I think I'll have another piece."

He chuckled. "I'll be sure and tell Sudie." He studied her as she leaned forward to cut another slice. Shadows played under her eyes and her movements were slow and deliberate, like those of someone physically tired. "So how was your first day?"

A small, Madonna-like smile played around her mouth, making her lips even more tempting. "Interesting."

He waited patiently while she quickly polished off the second piece of pie, but it soon became evident she wasn't going to volunteer any more information. She'd obviously had a hard day if she was too tired to talk.

"I came over to give you a tour of the barn, but you look like you're all tuckered out." She smiled and acknowledged the truth with a nod. "There's no hurry," he said, running his thumb over his mustache. "I just wanted you to be able to ride whenever you wanted. Waiting a couple of days till you're settled in won't make any difference. Is there any reason why all that," he indicated the rows of food, "can't wait until morning?"

"None at all. In fact, when you knocked at the door I was trying to decide between a shower or simply falling into bed. Since consuming those two pieces of pie, I've decided that bed wins hands down."

Adam rose and picked up their plates. "I'll skedaddle then."

He turned from putting the dishes in the sink to see Eve lever herself up from the table. Surprise reigned at the pang of tenderness he felt. He wanted to pick her up and tuck her into bed. But he was afraid that once he had Eve in his arms he'd be tempted to want more. Knowing what he was missing now made it all the more difficult for him to be chivalrous.

He hesitated before pushing open the storm door and looked

down at her. Her skin was so fair he could actually see the vein running alongside her temple. He'd never known anyone so full of contradictions: she appeared fragile, yet he'd seen that stubborn tilt to her chin proclaiming she'd accomplish what she set out to do. She had seemed naive, yet was astute enough to realize when he'd been putting on an act with his country routine. She didn't appear to have much self-confidence, yet she was more talented than even Alice as an artist.

When he realized she was staring at him with a perplexed look, he said softly, "You're a paradox, that's what you are." He leaned down and brushed his lips briefly against her forehead. "Good night."

Eve shut the door and, turning, leaned against it with her eyes closed. Absolutely useless to wish things were different, but oh, if they were. . . .

She opened her eyes to see Sheba sitting up and watching with her head cocked at an angle. "Oops."

She wrenched the door open and almost ran into the storm door in her haste. Pushing it open, she called, "Adam, you forgot Sheba." She heard his footsteps returning before he stepped into the light.

"So I did. Tell you what. Why don't you keep her with you at night? You're perfectly safe here, but she'd be company for you. Just let her out in the morning and she'll come home to be fed."

Wondering what he'd wind up sharing with her next, Eve nodded. "If you're sure, I'd enjoy having her."

She closed the door once more and knew that if things were different, if she were different and not who she was, Eve knew *exactly* what she'd like to share with Adam.

Seven

Eve came out of a deep sleep to the sound of Sheba barking. She sat up in bed and immediately the collie stopped, but proceeded to pace beside the bed, all the while whining.

Eve threw back the covers and got up. "What is it, girl?"

Sheba dashed toward the bedroom door and waited for her to

open it. Surely if there was a prowler the dog would still be barking. The thought had no sooner crossed Eve's mind than the grind of an engine starting up came through the window she'd left cracked open for fresh air. When she looked, she could see the pre-dawn darkness just beginning to fade. Enlightenment hit her at the same time Sheba barked once more. Adam must have been called out on another emergency.

"Is it Adam? Is that it, girl?"

The collie woofed and immediately disappeared down the hall. Following her and switching on the kitchen light, Eve found her pacing by the door. She wondered if Sheba would be able to catch him.

"All right," she said, opening the door. "But you might let your master know I don't think much of this new alarm system."

Outside, Eve could see that dawn was closer than she'd thought. She listened, heard the engine sound change as Adam apparently slowed down, then the slam of a door. Satisfied, she headed for the light switch, only to realize she wasn't really sleepy anymore.

She was hungry.

Deciding it must have something to do with all the fresh air she'd been getting the last two days while exploring, she decided to have an early breakfast. Tilly's hash browns and scrambled eggs sounded good. She dug out her cookbook. But after studying the recipe for several minutes, she frowned at the page.

"Chill baked-in-jacket potatoes, peel, shred to make four cups. Great!"

Not only did the recipe not tell her how many potatoes she needed, she'd be starving when they were ready to brown. The time it took to cook food had been another surprise, one her stomach didn't appreciate. Grumbling, she washed ten potatoes, stuck them in the oven and set the timer she'd purchased yesterday when she bought a new coffee maker.

Cutting a large piece of coffee cake to sustain her, she took the timer with her into the studio she'd set up at Adam's suggestion. She'd managed to finish two good sketches of Sheba since settling in and a passable watercolor. She considered trying to do one of the dog in oil for Adam.

Almost three hours later, Eve heard the sound of a car outside as she stared at the mountain of hash browns and scrambled eggs she'd prepared. Distracted, she moved toward the door and watched with amazement as her uncle climbed out of his Mercedes.

"Uncle Robb," she said, stepping outside hurriedly, "is anything wrong?"

"Not a thing." He came to a stop below where she stood by the door. "Unless you consider leaving me out of the loop of information about what's going on."

"But I asked Tilly to tell you. And since you found your way here, she must have done so."

"True," he agreed, "but an address and phone number hardly qualifies as an explanation of what you're up to." Eve recognized the steel underlying her uncle's pleasant tone. He wasn't going to be put off with a few throw-away lines. "Is this perhaps a bad time?"

Giving in to the inevitable, she smiled. "Not at all. As a matter of fact, your timing is perfect. Come in and join me for breakfast." She held the door open in invitation.

"You liked this place better than our cabin?" he asked as she headed toward the stove.

"I had my reasons." She busied herself with transferring food into dishes, then looked up to find him staring at her in fascination. She gathered two plates and silverware and, turning, handed them to him. "Would you set the table while I finish the toast?"

His shaggy brows, which had always reminded Eve of fat, fuzzy caterpillars, climbed even higher. "Of course."

Her uncle said nothing further until they were seated and he'd tasted everything, including the coffee. "My dear, you are to be congratulated. Everything is excellent."

A warm glow of satisfaction filled her. Thank you."

"But then, I can't say I'm surprised. In the past, you've managed to do whatever it is you set out to do." She looked at him in surprise. "Including indulging your father by getting an MBA and learning the ropes at Worldwide." He took another sip of coffee. "It remains to be seen what it is you've set your sights on now."

"Why don't we finish eating while the food is hot, then I'll try to answer your questions."

Shrugging trim shoulders beneath an elegant sports coat, he

ate sparingly while Eve filled her empty tummy. When at last he aligned his knife and fork across his plate and looked at her with raised brows once more, she'd made the decision to be completely honest with him.

"How much of a surprise would it be if I said I no longer have any interest in running Worldwide?"

His lips lifted in amusement. "Hardly any since I've sensed your . . . abstraction, shall we say, for some time."

Some of her tenseness dissipated at his words. "Then what do we do about Worldwide? I know you indicated your relief when the board nominated me as president, but would you consider taking over now?"

"My dear, I've never been more than an idea man. I left the running of things to first your father, then you. No," he shook his head of graying, sandy-colored hair, "being president has no appeal whatsoever."

Eve propped her chin on an up-raised palm. "That only leaves us with two options then, and selling to a competitor fills me with dread. I can't ignore the possibility of Worldwide being sold off in little pieces, and our people standing in an unemployment line."

"The other option being an employee buy out?"

She nodded. "How do you think they'd respond?"

Her uncle toyed with the handle of his cup. "That alternative was brought up at the time of your father's passing. When the power plays started getting intense with no clear winner, the board settled for nominating you as he wished." His hooded gaze lifted to hers as he said dryly, "One guess who was trying to get himself elected president, buy out or no."

Why wasn't she surprised? But the knowledge she'd been right about Richard's motivation for wanting to marry her still strung. "My, my, my. My ex-fiancé's been a very busy boy." Her lips tightened. "If he couldn't get control of the company one way, he simply tried another."

She looked at her uncle accusingly. "Uncle Robb, knowing what you did, why didn't you say anything when I told you Richard had asked me to marry him?"

He reached over and patted her hand. "For the simple reason, my dear, that he'd been successful in bringing you out of the funk caused by your father's death. And," he added when she twitched in impatience, "because you've always been a very bright girl. I didn't think it would take you long to catch on to Richard's ploy once you'd recovered all your faculties."

Eve ducked her head, unable to meet her uncle's eye as she asked, "Did you know about his . . . amorous activities? Did others?"

"I'm afraid discretion has never been Richard's strong suit." Hearing a chuckle, she raised her head. "What did surprise everyone was your putting an end to the engagement. Not knowing you as I do, I think they rather expected you to accept the situation. If you don't mind my asking, how *did* you find out?"

A smile began to form, and Eve realized with surprise she could be amused now by the incident. "Trapped in a bathroom stall at the Starlight fundraiser while his current *cher ami* discussed his technique with a friend."

"A rather crude way to learn the truth. I'm sorry."

"It may have been crude, but at least it shook me out of my lethargy. I'd been dithering for weeks about the engagement anyway. The more he pressed me to name a wedding date, the more panicked I became." At least Richard's taunt that she was responsible for his looking elsewhere remained her secret.

Her uncle beamed with approval. "See, I was right all along. Richard's indiscretion only accelerated matters."

"Will he be a problem if we try an employee buy out?"

His smile contained more than a hint of the determination that lay behind his calm exterior. "We have a decided advantage in the fact he's been a little overbearing since your engagement. All in all, I think he's taken a little too much for granted. Don't worry about Richard."

"The only thing that worries me is the feeling I've let you down."

"My dear, I realized many years ago that eventually the company would pass out of our hands. It's never been an obsession with me like it was with your father. I'm glad it's not one for you either." He looked at her from under the shelf of his brows. "And now, perhaps you can tell me what you're up to here."

"The truth is, I more or less fell victim to circumstances." Eve explained about her car and Adam's rescue. "It seemed churlish not to help out when all I was going to do at the cabin was vegetate. I may have decided I'm not cut out for corporate life, but I have to find something to do. Besides," she smiled faintly, "I find it reassuring that the people here accept me as I am. No one seems to want anything from me." Except Adam. And she had no intention of letting her uncle in on that impossibility.

His frown surprised her. "Do I understand correctly that no one knows your background?" At her nod, his frown deepened. "I was never enthusiastic about that particular part of your plan, including the second-hand car."

Eve stood and collected their plates. "I just wanted a chance to see how people would respond to me without my wealth coloring their reaction."

He followed her and refilled their cups as she rinsed the dishes. "I think there's more involved here than a broken engagement. Want to talk about it?"

She turned off the spigot and spoke after a long moment. "The night I broke off with Richard, I realized how isolated I'd become." She looked at her uncle directly. "There wasn't one friend I could call to talk to, woman-to-woman, and have her commiserate with me."

Sighing, she admitted, "It's my fault for letting things slide, then for letting Richard dictate my life. I find myself surrounded by people who are only interested in what I can do for them, but in all honesty I can't blame it all on him."

Her uncle picked up their coffee cups and nodded toward the table. "I'm aware it's been a long time since you truly had a life of your own. Probably since you agreed to go to graduate school." It went further back than that, but Eve shied away from the painful memories before college graduation.

"But, my dear, how realistic is it to build new relationships on a false premise?"

"I'll only be here a matter of weeks."

"So you say now. However, I've found that life can take unexpected turns and surprise us."

"If you're worried I may form a . . . permanent attachment for someone here, don't. You may as well know, Uncle Robb, that it's unlikely I'll ever marry." It was more than unlikely. However much she may have wished otherwise, Eve was positive about that fact. "All I have to do is settle on a new career, and I'll be fine."

"I want more for you from life than being *fine.*" Eve tensed for further probing, but after searching her gaze for several moments her uncle sighed. "Your father should have remarried after your mother's death. There'll be no one left when I'm gone, my dear. You'd be all alone in your old age. But," he said, rising to his feet, "I've trusted your good sense before. Why should I change now?" He smiled down at her. "Walk me to the car."

Eve heard another vehicle outside as she rose and her uncle's arm went around her. Apparently it was her day for visitors. But as they went through the door, she saw Adam backing up his truck. He apparently had decided not to bother her once he found someone's car already there.

"Adam, wait!" Turning to her uncle, she said, "Come meet my landlord."

His brows rose as the truck pulled back into the driveway. Adam's face beneath his Stetson looked carved in stone as he descended with Sheba at his heels. When Uncle Robb beamed at her, a sinking feeling started in Eve's stomach.

"Don't get the wrong idea," she muttered in a low voice, but she knew he'd already formed an erroneous opinion of why she had stayed.

Adam hadn't known he had a jealous bone in his body until an unpleasant sensation jolted through him at the sight of an older man's arm around Eve. Relief flooded him at discovering the dapper man to be her uncle. Shaking hands with him, he could see a slight family resemblance.

"Sorry, I didn't mean to interrupt."

"Not at all," Robb Sutton replied. "I was just leaving, but I'm glad to have a chance to thank you for helping Eve when her car broke down."

"It's nothing anyone else wouldn't have done, sir."

Her uncle's bushy eyebrows rose about two inches. "Sir, huh? I don't think I've had anyone call me that since I left the Navy." His eyes drilled into Adam's. "I think things are decidedly safer here, as well the people more polite, than in Chicago."

He shook hands with Adam again. "I'm glad I had a chance

to meet you. And your dog. At least now I'm reassured about Eve staying here. Old-fashioned of me, I know, but she's all I have."

He glanced sideways at her, shrugging as if in apology. Eve had a curious expression on her face until her uncle's final words, at which she leaned into his embrace.

"Better here than at some isolated cabin by herself, sir."

"Yes, I couldn't agree more." He kissed Eve on the cheek, saying, "I'll be in touch when I have some news, my dear. Meanwhile, don't hurry things."

Eyeing the Mercedes as it backed onto the road, Adam realized his usual reaction to the icons of wealth hadn't appeared. And it wasn't just because the guy was Eve's uncle; Robb Sutton's iron grip and penetrating gaze had told him a great deal about the man inside the fancy finery. He liked him . . . and his funny eyebrows.

He smiled at Eve and said, "I just dropped by to apologize for Sheba waking you so early this morning. I'd forgotten about that possibility when I decided she should stay the other night."

Eve wrinkled her nose. "I can't say I loved the wake-up call, but I have gotten a tremendous amount done." She looked up at him with bright, shining eyes. "Could I interest you in some breakfast?"

"You won't even have to twist my arm." Adam grinned with anticipation. "I haven't had anything to eat yet and I'm starved."

"I can even offer you a decent cup of coffee," she said, leading him inside with Sheba following. "It will just take a couple of minutes to scramble some more eggs."

He spotted the expensive European coffee maker right away and opened a cabinet door for a mug. A gift from her uncle; he obviously could afford it more easily than Eve. When he turned back, he noticed her scraping half a frying pan full of scrambled eggs into the garbage disposal.

"Your uncle wasn't hungry, huh?"

"He never eats very much, but that wasn't the problem. I'm still learning to judge recipes. Unless it calls for a specific amount, I always get it wrong."

When she turned on the burner under another frying pan and lifted the lid, he saw what she meant. There were enough hash browns left for a family, or a starving man.

"Well, I can help with this lot and if there's anything left, you've got a headstart on tomorrow's breakfast. As I'm sure you know, they'd be easier to reheat if you had a microwave. Most food is."

"Really? Maybe I'll get one then."

While she scrambled his eggs, he fixed toast and mulled over her comment about cooking. He decided he liked the homey intimacy of sharing a kitchen with her. When she backed into him as she bent over to check the burner flame, he turned and steadied her. Holding her much longer than necessary, Adam decided he liked it very much.

He glanced down at her trim figure, dressed in jeans and a paint-smeared sweatshirt, and said, "Bet I know what you've been doing this morning."

She lifted her head and stared at him, one hand still holding a spatula, the other resting lightly on his arm. Once their gazes connected, she became very still and time became protracted. It took every ounce of his will power not to pull her against him to once more sample those lovely lips. She had a very nice mouth, one usually spread in a generous smile, as generous as her nature.

Reminding himself he would be rewarded that much sooner if he didn't push her now, Adam dropped his hands and, turning, inhaled deeply. He grabbed the plate of toast and carried it to the table to give himself some breathing room.

Her voice, when it came at last, was distracted. "I'm sorry, I . . . I lost my train of thought. What did you say?"

Consoling himself with the knowledge that little miss City Girl wasn't unaffected herself, Adam looked over his shoulder. "I made a wild guess from the spots on your shirt that you'd been painting this morning."

"Yes," Eve said, returning to the scrambled eggs. "I was experimenting. It's been so long since I've worked with watercolors or oils that it was like starting all over." Adam literally could see the tension draining from her as she talked about washes, types of paper and brushes while he ate.

"I take it you like working at Alice's art store."

"Yes. I can't remember when I've had such fun, and she's *paying* me for it. I've decided to use my first paycheck to open an account at a local bank since I'm tired of her having to vouch for me every time I buy something."

He laughed as she wrinkled her nose, an echo of something she'd done two days ago but not when he first met her. Apparently she'd relaxed to the point of letting down her guard and becoming more natural.

"Since there's only one bank, you don't have much choice."

"That reminds me of something I was going to ask you about. I had lunch with Alice, Clarel and Connie the other day, and they were talking about the problem some people have had with getting financing through the bank to start new businesses." Her expression had grown perplexed. "Why does Hartwig make it so difficult? Doesn't he want the town to grow?"

Adam set down his coffee cup. "I think the real problem is that he stopped changing with the times somewhere in the seventies. We've had our difficulties, but I'm not being uncharitable when I say Hartwig's not had an original thought since I've been paying attention to such things."

He stood, gathered his dishes and carried them to the sink. "Enough about Hartwig. It's going to be a beautiful day, and there's a mare named Treasure I'd like you to meet. Care to go for a horseback ride?"

The smile he was coming to love lit up her face. "Just give me a minute to change my shirt."

On Saturday morning, Eve sat in the warm sunshine beside Adam's lake sketching three of the children whose faces she'd painted.

Jamie McKenzie and Ted Remson looked like expert fishermen with their cane poles, but Melissa McKenzie was another story. She couldn't keep her line there long enough to catch anything. So far, she'd only managed about five minutes of stillness before jerking the line to attract the fish's attention. Invariably her line caught on something unseen, losing her bait in the process. And also invariably, Brownie, the McKenzies' dachshund, barked full throttle. One of the boys managed to untangle the line for her until they tired of it and moved farther down the bank to fish in peace.

Eve had made a series of sketches of the children and the dog while listening to the children's chatter. She smiled at their ingenuousness as she bent over her sketchpad: Adam had offered them rides, and they asked him for riding lessons as well. With Brownie's excited cries ringing in her ears, she wondered again when Adam found time.

Suddenly, Brownie's barking turned to yelps of pain. Eve looked up to see Melissa's fishing line running from the end of her pole to the back of the dog's head. She scrambled up, reaching Brownie at the same time as Melissa.

Between sobs, she said, "It was an accident—" Brownie licked at her tears. "Honest, Miss Sutton—the line just *sprung* free—and caught Brownie." Sheba licked the little girl's face as well.

Eve tried to console her as the boys reached them. Ted held Brownie's head while Jamie examined the fish hook caught in a roll of fur on his neck.

Eve raised her voice to ask, "Can you get it out?"

"It's all the way through and back out again. I dunno. . . ."

"All right then. Do you have a knife?"

All three children stared at her, and Jamie's tanned face paled. "I don't think I—"

"Just cut the line above the hook, and we'll take him to Dr. Wagner to remove it."

Thank goodness she'd driven to the lake rather than riding Treasure since she planned to go for a horseback ride later with Adam. Jamie produced his knife, cut the line and picked up the whimpering dog. Eve put her arm around Melissa and hurried everyone to her car.

They reached the beautifully landscaped clinic quickly, Eve absently noting the details as she parked. They trouped into Adam's clinic, and Martha appeared almost at once.

"You brought the children, Miss Sutton?" she said after looking in vain for their parents.

Eve explained the fish hook, and Martha opened the door behind her. "Come this way, please." She led them down a short corridor with all the doors closed and, opening one, motioned them inside. "Put the dog on the examining table. The doctor will be with you shortly."

Sheba sat at Eve's side and stayed there while she tried to calm

Melissa. Noticing the boys' worried expressions, she assured them that Dr. Wagner would know just what to do. She only hoped they didn't have to wait long.

Fortunately for Eve's nerves, Adam opened the door and breezed in before five minutes had passed. She immediately calmed at his reassuring presence. He smiled at them and greeted Brownie, running his big hands soothingly over the dog. Scratching behind the dachshund's ears, Adam examined the hook without Brownie even being aware of it.

"This shouldn't take long. He's going to be fine," he told the children. He reached inside a cabinet and placed a tool on a nearby tray. Filling a syringe, he caught Eve's eye. "Think you can hold his head for me or should I get Martha in here?"

Melissa looked at her with tear-drenched eyes, and Eve swallowed. "Just tell me what to do."

She held Brownie's head, the boys each held his legs, just in case, and Melissa looked on with tears running down her cheeks. Adam made quick work of snipping off the barbed end of the hook, slipped it free, and washed the area with antiseptic.

When the dog whined, Eve, glancing at Adam from under her lashes, told the dachshund, "I know just how you feel."

Adam grinned at her beneath his mustache and gave the dog a shot of antibiotic. He put some pills in a paper envelope, gave them to Jamie and explained how to administer them. He also handed Melissa some dog biscuits and told her to keep Brownie quiet on the table for five minutes. Then he motioned Eve out of the room.

Sheba followed her and as soon as the door closed, she looked at Adam in fear. "Is there something you didn't want the children to know?"

"Not at all," he said, taking her arm, "but I think they can use a few minutes to calm down. I thought as long as you're here, I'd give you a quick look around."

She let out a little breath as he led her down the hall. "You shouldn't scare me like that. I'm still not over the shock of acting like a . . . like a parent, I guess. I don't think I could bear to tell Melissa if something had been wrong."

"You did very well," he said soothingly, sliding an arm around her. "I told you, you're a natural. But just to keep the record straight, I never lie to my patients' owners. Honesty is the best policy. Keeps false hopes from being raised and in the long run, it's easier on everyone."

Eve had been reveling in the reassurance of his arm resting along her shoulder, smelling the familiar woody scent of his aftershave and the starch that stiffened his white lab coat. But a sudden chill chased the warmth away. His words sunk in as he halted before a door marked surgery.

Adam returned her look quizzically. "You strike me as the straight arrow type. Don't you find honesty best?"

Eve could only nod, lost in the green depths of his gaze. But in her heart, she cringed at the scanty details she'd given him. He didn't really know anything about her, not truly. Given his antagonism toward wealthy people, would it make any difference in their friendship? If he found out, would he forgive her slight deception?

Eight

On Sunday morning, Eve worried at the thought of having deceived Adam while she worked on the painting of Sheba. It wasn't that she'd lied to him, she told herself; she'd just left wide holes in her background. But her uncle's words about building on a false premise echoed in her mind and unsettled her anew. Round and round her thoughts revolved until she realized that Adam would be arriving in half an hour.

She glanced down at herself to make sure she looked presentable. And remembered the load of laundry she'd started earlier that morning since she had no more clean clothes. She'd have to buy some more. She flung open the door to the basement and rushed down the stairs. But halfway to the bottom, her steps slowed to a halt at the sight of a foaming mass around the frontloaded washing machine.

"Oh, my stars!"

Eve stood staring at the mound of suds. What had she done wrong?

To save her last clean clothes, she stepped out of her shoes, jeans and blouse and tossed them toward the stairs. Grabbing a plastic pail, she waded through the suds and opened the door to the washing machine. More foam rested inside. She groaned as she realized she'd have to do the clothes again. Shutting the door and staring at the dial, she wondered if it would just rinse. Holding her breath, she turned the dial to the proper setting and pulled. The spray of tinkling water inside the machine lifted her sagging spirits.

For the next ten minutes, she bailed buckets of bubbles into the sink, swirled the mass around until it began to dissolve and dived back with her pail into the remaining foam. She found a pile of old towels to wipe up with and as the washing machine cut off, she stood grinning at a damp and cleaner floor—and one free of a speck of suds.

She pulled out pieces of clothing from the washing machine and threw them into the dryer. She noticed a pair of blue panties. Shrugging, she stuffed a pair of jeans inside and reached back into the washing machine. When the second pair of blue panties surfaced, then a blue bra tangled in a pair of jeans, Eve stared at them dumbfounded. Everything white was now blue. She'd stuffed everything together into the washing machine since there was so little laundry to do. She sighed; another lesson.

At the sound of Sheba barking at the kitchen door, Eve threw the rest of the clothes into the dryer, slammed the door and spun the timer. Then she flew to the stairs to rescue her clothes before Adam could catch a glimpse of her in her undies. By the time she'd dressed, stuffed her feet into her shoes and flew up the stairs, he was waiting at the door.

"All ready," she said, smoothing back hair she'd pulled into a ponytail that morning for their ride.

Having caught a glimpse of Eve only partially dressed, Adam swallowed and tried to banish visions of near-naked nymphs. He said the first thing that came to his mind. "You look about sixteen with your hair like that and your cheeks flushed. What have you been up to?"

The rosy tint of her cheeks deepened. "Just a few domestic chores."

If that was how women cleaned house, he'd been missing out

on something. A thought struck him as he led her to the truck. "Just how old are you . . . if you don't mind my asking?"

She laughed and climbed in. "I'm flattered, believe me. But I celebrated my thirtieth birthday earlier this year."

"And you're in such good condition for an old relic."

"It's the air here. Every day I can feel the years dropping away." He could have cheered at her enthusiasm; she *did* seem younger in spirit than when she'd first arrived. Maybe he wouldn't have so long to wait after all, he decided as she said, "So where are we going for these picnic supplies you mentioned?"

"To the Elegant Farmer," he replied and saw her smile. "I realize The Elegant Farmer may sound like a contradiction in terms, but I think you'll be pleasantly surprised."

When he pulled into a huge lot, Adam had to wait his turn to park. A nursery with colorful perennials, annuals and shrubs guarded the main entrance. Since it was Sunday, visitors thronged the well-known spot, as well as local residents. It amazed him then that, before they'd gone ten steps, someone hailed Eve. She smiled and waved, then her bright gaze danced over milling people to towering information boards, melon displays and the colorful nursery stock. No one, not even an actress—which Eve wasn't— could fake such a sustained level of interest in her surroundings. When he noticed her head turning constantly, he asked what she was looking for.

"That sign back there had a list of strawberry desserts, but I don't see any strawberries."

"Across the road," he said, jerking his thumb behind them. "That's where the fields are. People can pick berries themselves or buy as much as they want." He turned and nodded toward a small trailer with an adjoining area covered by an awning. "They also serve about six desserts that are sinfully delicious. We'll have some before we leave."

"Dessert *before* our picnic?"

He grinned. "I don't think ripe strawberries would survive being tossed about in a saddlebag. Come on," he said, pulling her after him, "let's find lunch."

They joined the line of people circulating slowly throughout the store, and he enjoyed watching Eve's expression while she scanned the merchandise. The Elegant Farmer offered everything from tourist knick-knacks to gourmet foods. He also noticed they were both greeted by name as they chose deli meats, various cheeses and two kinds of mustard.

While they waited for their fruit to be weighed, he said, "You seem to know a lot of people for being here such a short time."

Eve added some glistening grapes to their order. "Well, Alice carries more than just art supplies. People come in for all kinds of craft items. Do you like melon?" She showed him a package of sliced honeydew and cantaloupe and when he nodded, added the fruit to the basket he carried. "Then too, I scout around the stores after work. People are so friendly it's taken me all week to work my way through most of the town.

"That reminds me," she said over her shoulder. "You know that rock garden beside the kitchen door?"

"Used to be my grandmother's herb garden. Granddad kept it up for years, but let it go at the end."

"Mrs. Thompson mentioned it when she found out where I was living. I told her I didn't know dill weed from real weeds, and she's offered to come over tomorrow morning to help me sort it out. Do you mind?"

"Not at all. How do you know Granny Thompson?"

"I bought a quilt from her granddaughter at the fair, remember? I ran into her, Gloria I mean, the other day. One thing led to another, then Mrs. Thompson stopped in to see me at the store. It's amazing the things she knows.

"Learning about life here has been a revelation." Eve frowned as they moved forward in the check-out line. "I don't mean just small-town life as compared to the city. I'd guess the same things occur in suburbs and city neighborhoods. But moving between a suburb and Chicago for work, I never learned about either one. There was never time."

"Maybe that's the missing ingredient. Time. There's no question the pace of life is slower in a farming community compared to where you're from."

"Hmmm."

He was about to press her to name her preference as they left the store, but a farmer hailed him. Adam introduced her to Arnmunson and his family, then became interested in some symptoms his cow was displaying. But not so interested he lost track of Eve as she conversed with the man's wife and children. With half an ear, he listened to her draw out two shy teenage boys, make the younger girl laugh and the farmer's wife say more than five words. There was something about her, something different from other women he'd known, that everyone responded to. The only way he could describe it to himself was that Eve was like some exotic, imported plant that drew admirers compared to the wildflowers grown locally.

His interest had been piqued by a pretty girl whose clear, direct gaze accompanied a naivete in trusting strangers. Her lack of interest had aroused his male ego, and he'd been determined to make some sort of impression on her. It struck Adam that he'd been awfully determined to keep Eve around to prove his point. And yet, once he'd accomplished that, he'd slipped back into low gear. Then he reminded himself he was simply being a gentleman in giving her time to recover from her broken engagement. But to what purpose?

It wasn't like he could offer a woman like her anything. He still had several farms to recover before he could even think about any kind of permanent relationship. And Eve certainly wasn't ready for one. He was so startled at his thoughts that he almost missed Arn's puzzled look.

When he'd answered the man's questions, the farmer discreetly tried to hand him some money, but Adam waved it away. "Why don't we work out something in trade?"

"You have something in mind?"

"Several people have asked me about boarding horses this summer. Carl and my boys have enough to do already. Maybe your sons could do the morning stable routines and oversee the exercising. Goodness knows, there are enough horse-mad kids to do the actual exercising with supervision."

"Ya, I think that is possible."

"Good. I'll give you a call."

Afraid Arn might become more effusive in his thanks, he separated Eve from them as quickly as possible. It seemed the most natural thing in the world to throw his arm around her shoulders as he led her across the highway. But settled on bales of hay in the shade of the awning, it turned out she'd been as attuned to his conversation as he had been hers.

"If you don't mind my asking," she said after several bites of strawberry shortcake, "what is it you're working out in trade?"

He finished swallowing a mouthful of sundae and pushed his hat back on his head. "Oh, Arn's just had a run of bad luck. Since he needs all the cash he can lay his hands on and I need someone to do stable chores, it seemed the simplest solution to settling his vet bill."

"Why is it I get the feeling this isn't the first time you've done this?"

He looked at her sweet smile and, for the first time, felt he could share some of the things he kept bottled up inside. She was so darned easy to talk to. "I wish it were possible to go back to the days when everyone traded for what they needed. Kept everyone on a par, more or less. But," he sighed, "that's not possible. Today when you want to expand your business, your farm or your dairy, as Arn did, you go to the money man. It's quicker, but dangerous, too. Sometimes those dreams are put in jeopardy by the money man's rules."

"By money man, do you mean a banker?" At his nod, her spoon halted on its swing to her tempting mouth. "And by banker, you mean Hartwig specifically, don't you?"

"Yeah." He pushed his empty dish aside. "Don't get me wrong. Banking is a business and I know they have to have rules, but Hartwig's terms are always just a little stickier, a little harsher than elsewhere." Adam broke off in exasperation, as usual feeling his blood pressure rise at Emery's tactics.

"Then why don't they go elsewhere to another bank?" Then Eve's knitted brows smoothed out as she immediately said, "Oh, because they already have a mortgage with his bank and it's easier. . . ."

"Yeah. He's made himself the richest man in the county. He could afford to forego his pound of flesh for the poor devils who *really* have to work for a living, but he never does. He never gives them a break. It's that needless grinding of souls and pride into the dirt I can't forgive."

Eve knew he was thinking of his father and grandfather. Especially his grandfather. She'd learned that Ramsey Wagner had worn himself down by doing the work of three men trying to rid himself of debt. How much had his life, or others, been shortened by Hartwig's greed?

"What about some type of cooperative for financial assistance?" she asked. "Has anyone ever thought of trying to start one?"

"It's been discussed." He resettled his hat and rose. "Unfortunately, in order for it to be of any use, there'd have to be an existing cash reserve and we've had too many years of drought and disaster. Everyone is stretched to the limit. We need a couple of good years or. . . ."

"Or?"

His grin was mocking as he looked down at her. "Or a fairy godmother. Come on. Let's forget about money matters and blow the cobwebs out of our minds with a ride."

As much as she enjoyed flying in Adam's wake astride Treasure along fertile or fallow fields and through orchards adrift in blossom petals, Eve couldn't quite dismiss their discussion.

Money. She was beginning to learn that a great many people here had money worries, but she hadn't known it. They simply went on with their lives, grateful for the good times and struggling through the bad.

How long had it been since she'd taken the time to enumerate her own blessings, to realize there *were* positive aspects to her life? Especially here. A sense of growing competency in her artistic ability, her new friends providing a warm feeling of acceptance, her escalating confidence in handling Alice's daughter, Sheba's companionship, and Adam. . . .

What did she get from Adam?

At that moment, he looked back over his shoulder to check on her as they raced through a grassy meadow. She saw his eyes blaze with approval for keeping up with him and the now familiar grin stretched under his mustache before he resettled his hat and faced forward once more. Beneath his Stetson, his hair curled over the edge of his collar.

She felt such a rush of . . . excitement, expectancy at the first thought of him before she caught herself. But with Adam around, there was no doubt her enjoyment of things increased tenfold.

She realized suddenly it was the first time since college that she'd had a male *friend*. The relationship she'd slotted him into, the only one she'd mentally allow, was completely different from those of her former boyfriend, fiancé or fellow-workers. The hour or so Adam allotted for their daily rides provided not only much needed exercise after sitting and sketching or painting for so long, but a sounding board for her thoughts and feelings about the people she encountered.

Adam slowed as the line of trees before them grew larger, and she drew abreast of him. Sheba reappeared in their wake, apparently having lost interest in whatever creature she'd been chasing. Their pace slowed to a trot and then a walk as they entered the edge of a woods that covered the ridge.

It immediately became cooler, and Eve laughed in delight. "I didn't think I was ever going to be able to complain about being too warm, but this shade feels wonderful."

"If you think this is nice, wait till you see the surprise I have for you."

"What?" She remembered the half-full saddlebags he'd produced but wouldn't let her peek into before packing their lunch. She looked at him expectantly.

He leaned over and flicked a finger down her nose. "Now if I told you, it wouldn't be a surprise."

She couldn't remember the last time she'd been teased . . . by anyone. Smiling with sheer happiness, she looked back the way they'd come as she felt the angle of their incline increase. They were higher than she'd realized. "Are we leaving the valley for this surprise?"

"Nope." Adam nodded to the right. "This ridge broadens into Glacier Pass, but we're staying on this side of it. We don't have much farther to go."

The trees became denser and he took the lead, winding through the towering trees on no path Eve could discern. She heard the trickle of water tumbling over rocks before she spotted the small stream. Adam changed direction and continued to climb the hillside along the brook. At last he stopped.

It wasn't until she came alongside him that she could see the small sunny meadow stretching before them. Beyond it lay the length of Adam's valley. From here you could see all the undulations of the land as it rose and fell in gentle swells.

Only from here could you see the colors all at once: bright green for the meadows, deeper variations of green from the surrounding trees, brown for the newly plowed fields, and a patch of blue indicated the lake at the lower, far end of the valley. The deep red of the huge barns made a joyful splash of color.

"It's lovely."

"Yes." At his quiet agreement, Eve saw that his gaze roamed the breadth and length of his valley. "It's different in every season and yet just as spellbinding. When my batteries need recharging, I come up here and say thanks to my ancestors. Bless them every one."

"Was it always like it is now?"

"Not by a long shot," Adam told her as he dismounted and held her horse so she could join him. "When my ancestors came here to homestead, this was still virgin forest. Gustave Wagner and his brother were already in Chicago when this became known as Wisconsin Territory."

He staked the horses so they could graze. "They'd been here two years already when some of the surrounding towns were founded." He stood beside Eve once more, the breeze whipping her light fragrance to him, and he longed to take her into his arms. Instead, he continued, "The valley had everything they needed: trees for wood, springs for water, as well as the lake, game aplenty, and friendly Indians.

"And speaking of springs," he took her arm and turned her away from the valley, "let me show you my surprise."

He led her back into the shade of the trees and the murmur of the brook. What she saw instead was the beginning of the stream, a rock-lined pool of water that bubbled up out of the ground.

She knelt on its mossy ledge and cupped her hands in the water. Sheba licked at the falling drops, then padded to the stream to drink. "It's like ice."

"Gustave found this and lined the pool and the beginning of the stream with rocks so it wouldn't wear the ground away. There are several springs that feed the lake." He reached past her and plunged into the shadowy water up half the length of his arm. When his hand rose, it held a dripping, dark-green bottle. "I put this here yesterday so our wine would be cold for lunch. Come on."

Adam helped her to rise, then handed her the chilled bottle while he removed the saddlebags from his horse. Sheba had caught the scent of something again and disappeared on its trail. Following him to the edge of the clearing, Eve looked around and caught the gleam of metal through the trees and bushes. When she turned back to ask him about it, he'd pulled a blanket from one side of the saddlebag.

She helped him spread it and asked, "What is that fence over there?"

"The family graveyard. I'll show you after we've eaten." When he reached down to pick up the saddlebag, she saw two wine-glasses resting beside it. "Sudie bet me they'd get broken, even with the blanket for protection."

For the first time, she wondered about the women in Adam's life and felt a pang he might have shared all this with them. "Sounds like you've done this before."

"Not me. But there's a first time for everything. Why don't you get the food out while I open the bottle?"

He looked so pleased with himself, she couldn't help smiling as she unwrapped their purchases. "You mentioned friendly Indians before. What kind?"

"Potawatomies. The Sioux had already been pushed to the Mississippi. Even though friendly, the Potawatomies were curious and hung around. My early grandmother left a diary telling of their begging for food or clothing. More dangerous were the bears and wolves."

"Bears?" Eve looked over her shoulder into the woods.

"Don't worry, City Girl. They're long gone," he said, handing her a glass. "What shall we drink to?"

"Ancestors and new beginnings."

"Very appropriate." He touched her glass with his, and she sipped the cool, crisp white wine. "So how's it going? The new beginning, I mean."

"Better than I hoped. My car breaking down where it did was the best piece of luck I've ever had. I can't remember when I've enjoyed myself more."

"Me neither." Before she could think how to follow that up, he said, "Think you like it well enough to stay around a while?"

"Well, I have three weeks left." At the realization of how quickly one week had slipped away, she paused, the knife she'd been using to spread mustard for their sandwiches drooping in her hand. "I just remembered that old saw, 'Time flies when you're having fun.' I'm going to hate to leave."

"Then why go?"

Nine

Startled, Eve's gaze flew to his. Adam lay across the blanket, the food between them, but the angle of his body brought his head close to hers. He'd removed his Stetson, and the sun filtering through the trees in patches warmed the honey color of his hair. But it was his expression, dead serious, that caught her attention. Beneath his mustache, no smile lurked to tease a response from her.

Eve wet her lips. "My leave of absence is only for a month."

"And then what?"

"I . . . I go back home."

"Why? What's there for you besides a job?" When she just stared at him, he said, "You as much as admitted the first night I met you that you don't even like your job anymore. You haven't shown me any of your work, but I know you've been painting. I knew the first time I saw you drawing that you were good. You should give yourself a chance to develop that talent. You can do that here."

Her heart seemed to swell at his words, and a knot formed in her throat. Adam was the first man to appreciate her as a person with an innate gift. Not for her money, not for what she could provide, because he didn't know that Eve Sutton. He liked her simply for herself.

"What are you suggesting?"

"Just that I think you should consider making Brighton your home. You can continue to live in my granddad's house while you paint. You have a job for several more months if you want, maybe longer the way Alice talks. We're friends. Friends help one another."

Eve's heart hammered with confusion, joy, trepidation, hope, fear and anticipation. Her responses were so conflicting, she felt dizzy for a moment and bowed her head. She tried to sort through the emotions swamping her. Surprise was there, surprise at finding herself wishing for just a moment that he'd also volunteered undying love. Relief soon followed in a burst of practicality, relief because she wouldn't have known what to do with such a declaration anyway.

Maybe she wouldn't have to leave Adam—and everyone else. And she smiled.

"Ah, that means you agree, right?"

Lifting her head, his direct, candid gaze caught hers. His honesty deserved the same. "Yes, at least in part."

She had to assert her independence without presuming a possible attraction on Adam's part. She only hoped her growing attraction to him hadn't been visible, especially to him. "The only way I can remain in your grandfather's house is if I pay you rent. I *can* afford it, you know."

"You may be able to afford it, City Girl, but there's no way you're going to change horses in midstream. We had a deal, remember? A few home-cooked meals for me, and you pay the utilities." A grin spread slowly, doing funny things to her stomach. "I wouldn't complain any though if you wanted to pay up on that part of your agreement."

"Oh! Uh, of course." Thinking a few seconds, she bravely volunteered, "How about in a couple of days? I have to plan the menu, shop. . . ."

"Whatever you say."

"Well then, there's just one more thing."

He lifted sandy brows in inquiry just as she realized she didn't have the faintest idea of how to keep him from encroaching on her space, if romancing her was his intention. He reached for some grapes and watched her as he popped them into his mouth, a mouth that could work such miracles.

"Um. . . ." Since nothing brilliant offered itself, she drew a steadying breath and said, "I just wanted to be sure you understood that—that being my landlord didn't also—I mean, that you didn't think—"

Reaching over, he removed the mustard-wielding knife from her nerveless fingers. Before she realized how it happened, Eve found herself tugged down until she lay head to head with Adam, her hands enfolded in his big, work-callused ones.

"What you mean, City Girl, is that you're warning me off in your ladylike way." His eyes reflected only amusement, which grew as she felt her embarrassment spread up her neck to warm her cheeks. "And I accept the boundaries."

She could only stare at him in mute surprise.

"I promise I'll behave like a gentleman, eat your delicious meals, and enjoy your company with no strings attached." A frown passed over his tanned features a moment and he said, "You just let me know if anyone gives you any trouble. I sort of feel responsible for you and all," he added when she opened her mouth at last to protest. "And to seal our bargain—"

Without warning, his lips covered hers. His mouth was warm, his mustache a delicious tickle of sensation that joined the flood assailing her. She enjoyed it too much to protest. When he finally released her, Eve experienced the fascinating feeling of having a champion and protector. She felt truly rich for the first time in her life.

Her old nemesis echoed at the thought. Money. She remembered the holes she'd left in her background that formed Adam's erroneous impressions. Her courage failed her for a moment. The gift of her liberating response to him was so new, so fragile, she hesitated to put his goodwill to so immediate a test.

But if he was her friend, surely learning she was wealthy would make no difference. She drew back so she could see his response as she told him. "Remember when I said you didn't really know me? Well—"

"I figure," he said, nibbling at her lips, "that we have plenty of time now to solve that problem."

What he did with his mouth was titillating and should be outlawed. She'd never experienced such a rush from a simple kiss.

He wasn't sure how it had happened, but Adam found he couldn't leave her mouth alone. He'd meant to tease her with a light, quick kiss to reaffirm their bargain. And, he acknowledged, to also let her know that while he understood her boundaries, that didn't mean he wouldn't push at them from time to time. He'd probably sounded like a Neanderthal offering to be her protector. But the thought that someone else might also share those home-cooked meals and enjoy her company had him again wishing to put his stamp on her.

When she surfaced from his kiss, Eve tried again. "But—"

"If it makes you feel any better, we'll use these next three weeks to fill in the bigger blanks. That was your original timetable to leave." He punctuated his words with quick light kisses under her chin and down her throat. "I promise to give it my utmost attention."

Her attention focused on the spiraling tension he aroused in her as he made a circuit of her neck with his mouth. While his lips seduced, his mustache provided a counterpoint of texture. She felt the hardness of his teeth against her fragile skin as she shivered, the softness of his hair curling over his crisp collar when she reached for him, the strength of his body yet the gentleness of his hands as they roamed over her. The heat surprised her. An ache started deep inside that seemed to grow as—

Sheba barked close to her ear. Then the collie nosed her way between their faces, licking them each in turn.

With an oath, Adam tried to push the dog away and at the same time keep Sheba's claws from hurting Eve as she pawed at them. Sheba obviously thought it a terrific new game and barked harder. When he used his knee to block her, she jumped on his back. He hunched over Eve to protect her, yelling at the dog. The more he tried to hide her from Sheba, the more excited the collie became.

When Eve first felt something tug at her hair, she thought it was Adam . . . until she realized both his hands were occupied. The tug came again as Sheba whined next to her ear. She dissolved in helpless laughter.

When Adam felt Eve quaking beneath him, he drew back in quick alarm. Sheba bounded in and licked at him, but he heard the wonderful sound of bubbling laughter next to his ear.

Sheba stuck her cold nose against his neck and whined before she nosed him aside to reach Eve. Another ripple of laughter met her assault. Eve's safety assured, he began to see the humor of the situation and started to chuckle. Her merriment became contagious.

Unfortunately, Sheba took their laughter as a signal the game was still on and tried to get between them again. Eve rolled when she felt the collie's foot on her head and something wet stuck to her cheek. It smelled like cantaloupe. . . .

"Adam, the food! Get her off."

"Sheba . . . heel!"

Gasping for breath, he made it to his knees. With Sheba sitting at his side, but still looking anxiously at them, he glanced to where Eve hovered over the blanket, her body protecting their picnic lunch. He sputtered, trying to hold his laughter in, afraid he'd set Sheba off again.

He stood and, calling Sheba to his side, walked her to where the horses grazed. "Sheba, stay!"

He returned to the blanket and helped Eve sort out their lunch. Fortunately, only a few pieces of fruit had been lost and their wineglasses spilled. Their glances met and both chuckled.

She looked so delectable smiling at him that he leaned over to steal another kiss. A hairsbreadth away, they both heard the familiar whine and looked over their shoulders. Sheba, about a foot away, was inching toward them on her belly.

The next day when they returned home from their now daily ride, they found Adam's housekeeper just leaving. Eve went to meet her while he unsaddled the horses.

Sudie began shouting to her before she covered half the distance from the barn. "Hi. Have a good time?"

"Great. There's so much to see." And today Adam had kept things strictly platonic. She hadn't decided yet if she was greatful or disappointed. "Over the last two days, Adam's showed me the various farms, fruit groves, the lake and a bog, the family graveyard and several springs."

"Should have known that boy would show off his valley. If he has a weakness, this land is it."

"He has a right to be proud," she said, leading the way into the kitchen. "It's a wonderful heritage. Would you like some iced tea?" She'd already removed the pitcher of tea from the refrigerator before she thought to ask, "Was there something special you wanted?"

Eve poured the tea, fidgeting under Sudie's curious gaze. When she handed over the glass of iced tea, she thought she saw speculation in the housekeeper's bird-like manner. But Sudie briskly said, "Now here I am forgetting why I came over, although I'd meant to stop by to see you anyway. But before I get sidetracked again, you had a phone call. Said he was your uncle. He tried Adam's house when he couldn't reach you here."

"Uncle Robb?"

"That's his name," Sudie said, unfolding a piece of paper she'd taken from her ever-present apron pocket. "Robb Sutton. Said to tell you that the foundation idea will work." She handed the note to Eve.

"That's wonderful news." Eve had called her uncle to see if they could set up some sort of foundation to fund new businesses and to start the paperwork. "Did he want me to return his call?"

"No, he said he'd get back to you in a day or two. If you don't mind my asking, what's this foundation thing about?"

Eve led the way over to the comfortable seating by the fireplace and told her what she'd heard about local women's difficulty in getting loans. "I thought about this foundation that specializes in entrepreneurs and asked my uncle to find out some details, how to apply and so forth."

So forth covered a lot of ground, but she wanted the foundation to remain anonymous and have no direct connection to her.

"Well, glory be! That'd show Emery a thing or two, wouldn't it?"

Eve smiled. "I certainly hope so. I think he's had things his way long enough." She sipped her iced tea and had another idea. "Sudie, would you like to join us for lunch tomorrow? Knowing everyone the way you do, perhaps you could contribute some ideas we haven't thought of yet. So far, it's just been sort of pie in the sky."

"Sure. Anything to ruffle Emery's feathers. I'll wear my best bib and tucker." Sudie noticed her quick frown and asked what was the matter.

"I just remembered that I need to go shopping. I'll have to try and squeeze it in somehow. I do laundry, but I seem to keep running out of clean clothes."

Sudie snapped her fingers. *"That's* what I forgot to tell you about the other day." She tilted her head and said, "Though if you've already washed, you probably discovered for yourself how cantankerous that old machine is."

"If you mean it wasn't all my fault that I created a super bubble bath, then I'm grateful. What's the secret?"

"Come on. I'll show you."

But they made it only to the door of the basement when Adam entered the house. "Oh, Adam," Sudie said, patting her apron pocket. "I almost forgot I took a message for you too when I dropped off your dinner. Langley's having some problem or other and wants you to give him a call."

He sighed. "There goes the rest of my evening. Okay if I use your phone?" he said, turning to Eve.

She waited with Sudie while Adam made his call and could tell by his conversation that he'd have to visit Langley's farm. Though she was sorry, she told herself it was just as well. Things had been moving much faster than she'd believed possible. Though there'd been no repeat performance of yesterday's episode, she'd caught him looking at her several times. Surely it was her own imagination that provided a yearning quality to those stolen glances. Wasn't it? A breathing space would give her time to put things back in perspective.

Under Sudie's watchful eye, Adam kept his farewell circumspect. Then she followed his housekeeper down the basement stairs to learn the intricacies of the washing machine and dryer.

Late the next morning, Eve hurried into Alice's shop carrying the watercolor she'd done of Sheba.

"Oh, it's lovely," Alice said. "I should have known you'd be this talented. What else have you done?"

"I've started on an oil painting of Sheba also, but my sketchbook is about half full."

Alice made her retrieve it from the car. Eve stood, shifting from foot to foot while her friend studied the sketches. As she continued to flip the pages, Eve could see with growing satisfaction that her images had improved with practice. Alice studied the series of the children done last weekend and sighed.

"I can tell from these drawings that you'd be good at landscapes, but I think your forte is going to be portraits."

"But I've never studied portraiture."

Alice smiled. "I don't think you have to. Look," she said, pointing to the drawing of Melissa baiting her fish hook. "You've only used a few lines, but I can recognize who it is. The same with these others." She flipped back to the original drawing of Sheba and held it beside the finished watercolor. "See what I mean? If you're this talented, you don't have to study. You just do it."

"I did the painting for Alex. Would you teach me how to mat and frame it?"

"Of course. It's not difficult, just time-consuming." She picked up the painting and moved into the back room. "I'll give you a demonstration on matting now, and you can practice on some scraps. When I finish at school, we can start on a frame."

They'd worked together for several minutes when Alice said, "Would you let me mat some of your drawings for display out front?"

Eve looked up from where she was practicing how to cut a beveled edge. "I guess so, but why?"

Alice grinned. "Because once those kids' parents see what you can do, you'll probably be given a commission to do some portraits."

A breath of surprise escaped, and she tried to tamp down her rising excitement. "You think I'm that good?"

Alice laughed and gave her a hug. "I *know* you're that good. Come on," she said, gathering up her daughter, "it's time to meet the others for lunch. Wait till I tell them."

Fifteen minutes later, Alice raised her glass in a toast. "To our resident portrait *artiste.*"

Eve swallowed as Sudie, Connie and Clarel raised their glasses in a salute. To dissipate some of her nervousness, she laughed. "Aren't you rushing things just a little?"

"No false modesty," Connie declared. "If Alice says you're talented, that's good enough for me."

Eve glanced around Wickman's Tavern and Restaurant. Crowded now with construction workers and telephone linemen drinking beer with their pizza, as well as store owners hunched over quick sandwiches, the century-old stone building vibrated with noise.

Sudie followed her track and said, "The town's not only going to survive, it's growing."

"Speaking of growing," Connie turned to Eve, "what's this Sudie mentioned about some foundation giving away money to start new businesses?"

She laughed. "They're not exactly giving it away, but it should be easier for entrepreneurs to open businesses." She gave them the same explanation she'd given Sudie and hoped there would be a way to help the wives of some of the men Adam felt so concerned about. She looked around at the women who'd become her friends. "I asked Sudie to join us so we could pool our knowledge about the types of businesses that might be possible. Search your memories for things people might have mentioned an interest in."

Once they started reminiscing, they quickly came up with six names and types of businesses. Although Connie worked in Milwaukee, she'd picked up a handful of clients locally within the last year. She thought several of them might be possibilities.

"Wait a minute," she said. "I know from experience how difficult it is to get a new business off the ground. So does Clarel. We should get these people together and talk to them, let them know what lies ahead."

Clarel said, "People starting a business should have an accountant and an attorney, as well as some sort of business plan. Otherwise, they increase their chances of failing."

Connie nodded thoughtfully. "One of my clients here is an attorney. Marilyn Grant. She quit to have her first child last year. I wonder if she'd be interested in lending a hand?"

"I could help with advice about marketing and business plans," Eve offered.

By the time they'd finished lunch, their enthusiasm and excitement had grown. Sudie had offered to contact the women who'd expressed a business interest, and Alice offered her store as a meeting site.

"Goodness, look at the time," she said. "I have to fly."

"Before you go," Sudie laid a hand on her arm, "I wanted to

ask your advice. Adam's thirty-fifth birthday is coming up. Do you think we could pull off a surprise party?"

Alice grinned. "I think it would only be fair since he and Fisk pulled one on me a few years ago for my thirtieth. The three of us will put our heads together." She flashed Eve a conspiratorial smile, kissed her daughter good-bye and left.

Eve flushed at automatically being included in anything that included Adam, but she felt grateful, too. None of these people had ever treated her like an outsider.

Sudie accompanied her as she walked back to the store, pushing Karen in her pram. "I was wondering something. Is this foundation thing only to help women?"

"No, I don't think so. Why?"

"I wondered if there was any way to help Fisk with his landscaping business."

"I thought he was a construction worker."

"He was forced into it when his folks lost their farm years ago, but that boy loves the land almost as much as Adam." Sudie looked at her, puzzled. "I thought Adam showed you all over the valley. Didn't you see the tree farm?"

"Tree farm. . . . Oh, yes. There was an area he showed me ingeniously watered by a spring on the side of a hill. Is that what you mean?"

Sudie shook her head. "Should have known that boy wouldn't toot his own horn. Adam loaned the land to Fisk to grow shrubs and saplings since he couldn't afford to buy or even rent land with Alice saving to start a new business. He's been doing landscaping on the side for about five years now and wants to do it full-time. Seems to me with all these homes going in, some of which he's already picked up as clients, it'd be a natural. You've seen his work. What do you think?"

"Seen his work? Where?"

"Why, around Adam's house for one. And the clinic. Since Adam wouldn't take any rent for the land, Fisk insisted on landscaping both. Anything around town that looks like it's been spruced up lately is probably his work."

"Alice never said anything."

And neither had Adam. He might have his blind spots, like his distaste for wealthy people, but he didn't stand around and bemoan his fate or those of others in need. He did something about it. She'd have to work harder at helping also.

"Sudie," she said with rising excitement, "can you get Fisk to call me at the store? If he's already in business, it should be easier for him to come up with figures and a basic plan to satisfy the foundation." She'd make sure of it. "I'd like to do something to help them. They're such nice people."

"All right. We'll let Alice help us plan Adam's surprise party, and maybe we can surprise her, too."

Asked where the party would be held, the housekeeper said, "Ordinarily, I'd suggest the grounds of Ramsey's house. But with the amount of time Adam's been spending there lately, I don't know how much we could hide."

At her quick flush, Sudie smiled and patted her arm. "I don't mean to tease you. If I had my druthers, I'd choose the problem of a site for the birthday party over Adam finding someone to settle down with."

"Oh, but it isn't what you think! I mean, Adam and I are just friends."

"Why, don't you like him?"

"Of course I do. But—"

"Hmmm." Sudie studied Eve as she unlocked the door to the craft shop and flipped the sign in the window. "You have to do what you think best, of course, but if I were you I'd trust my instincts."

Ten

Eve glanced at her watch and swore under her breath. She'd forgotten to set the timer when she put the pie shell in the oven to brown. For a moment she wondered why she'd thought it a good idea to invite Adam to dinner this evening. Her proposed menu of chicken breasts in mushroom and tarragon cream sauce, asparagus souffle, salad, and Adam's favorite pie had seemed so simple in theory. But as she was learning, nothing about cooking was simple.

She quickly stirred cream of asparagus soup already combined with melted cheese into beaten egg yolks for a souffle. Setting aside the pan, she stuffed her hands into oven mitts and removed the pie crust from the oven. She groaned when she saw it was more than lightly browned as she'd heard Sudie say was the secret to avoiding a soggy pie crust. Oh well, once she'd filled it with strawberries and rhubarb, who'd know the difference? It was bound to soften up some.

Setting it aside to cool, Eve reread the recipe Tilly had given her and went back to putting the souffle together. She chuckled, remembering her housekeeper's surprise that she was cooking at all, let alone a whole dinner. Once the souffle mixture rested safely in the casserole, she taped on a paper collar and slid it carefully into the lower oven. Adam would be here in an hour, and she'd have time to brown the chicken breasts as he put together the salad ingredients she'd already prepared. That left only finishing the pie and the cream sauce.

Unfortunately, the top crust proved difficult and she rerolled it several times. She was perspiring by the time she was satisfied and popped it into the upper oven, then put together the cream sauce to warm at the last minute. Time to clean the kitchen and take a quick shower before Adam showed up.

As it was, she had barely reentered the kitchen when she heard Adam's arrival through the screen door he'd recently put in place. A long, slow whistle startled her, and she turned to face him standing in the doorway. A smile of appreciation spread as he took in the one summery dress she'd brought with her.

"Do you realize this is the first time I've seen you in anything other than pants? Wow! It was worth waiting for," he declared as he set a sack on the counter. Wrapping his arms around her, he lowered his head.

The jolt Eve had felt at the sight of Adam was nothing to the one sizzling through her as his kiss lingered and deepened. She'd decided to go along with his playful attitude toward their friendship. What did she know? Maybe everyone behaved this way. It was certainly innocent enough, and she enjoyed the sensations rushing through her at his gentlemanly but tempting kisses too much to resist them. His arms finally loosened and he drew back.

"Wow!" she said, repeating his last words. "That was worth waiting for."

"The penalty for mockery is another kiss."

His lips covered hers again, and Eve became aware of the explosive warmth blooming inside her. As Adam lifted her against him, a muffled whine grew louder. He lifted his head at a loud bark and turned toward the screen door with her still in his arms. Now that Sheba had their attention, she scratched at the door and whined again.

"I'm going to start leaving that dog at home," he threatened.

Eve wriggled free and went to open the door. "You wouldn't be so cruel."

He muttered under his breath. Maybe he'd better not. At least with Sheba around he was assured of not being able to take things too far too fast. His good intentions seemed but a faint memory lately around Eve. "Probably not."

He withdrew the bottle of wine from the bag he'd brought and opened a drawer looking for the corkscrew. "Something smells good," he said, as Eve opened another drawer and took out an apron.

"No peeking," she warned. "It'll spoil the surprise."

He spotted two wineglasses on the counter and poured the chilled white wine. When he turned to give Eve hers, disappointment settled at finding her enveloped in one of Sudie's neck-to-hem aprons. "To surprises," he said, clicking his glass with hers.

Eve removed the ingredients she'd prepared for the salad from the refrigerator. "Would you put this together while I brown the chicken breasts?" At his nod, she added, "And as much as I like your distractions, would you please wait until I get dinner on the table? Tilly said that timing is everything."

When she finally returned to the stove, she saw with dismay that the cream sauce was bubbling away at a full boil. Oh well, she'd just have to hope it'd be okay.

Three minutes later the timer went off with a *ding*. "Darn," she said, reaching for the oven mitts. "The chicken's not ready yet."

"A few minutes won't make that much difference."

Opening the oven door, she withdrew the casserole dish and placed it carefully on a burner of the stove to keep it warm. "With a souffle, I'm not so sure."

"I thought you said you didn't know how to cook."

"Anyone can follow a recipe."

making her hunch her shoulder. "As I said, it's only a small delay. Besides, I think I can put the time to good use."

His lips trailed up the side of her neck and along her jaw before she pulled away. "You don't understand. I feel like such a fool." She looked miserable. "I was so smug about being able to follow a recipe."

"Hey, look at me."

When she did, his gaze was so full of tenderness it almost stopped her breath. It curled her toes instead. Without realizing she did so, she reached for him. Their lips met and Sheba started barking, but they ignored her. After a minute, their lips separated but remained close, their foreheads touching instead.

"If I haven't told you so lately, you're one fine lady with an abundance of gifts. With a little help from Sudie, you can learn to cook, too."

"Oh, Adam. I'm not sure I can learn to do anything right."

He grinned beneath his mustache. "Then I'll just have to set about reassuring you with my specialty, won't I? You were a quick study the other day."

Color bloomed in her cheeks, but before he could take advantage of the moment, he heard the spattering of the frying chicken.

"Whoops." He hurried into the kitchen, saying, "I almost burned our dinner. He flipped the meat and lowered the flame under the frying pan, then picked up the wine bottle from the table. As he poured more wine into their glasses, he noticed a gaily wrapped package on the coffee table. "What's that?" he asked, handing Eve her glass.

She managed a smile as she picked up the package and handed it to him. "For you."

He grinned and ripped the paper apart. His grip tightened on the frame when he caught sight of the watercolor. He recognized the familiar expression on Sheba's face, the same one he'd seen in one of Eve's sketches. She'd painted it for him; she'd remembered and gone to the trouble of giving him something he'd treasure.

"You couldn't have given me anything that would please me more."

Adam kissed her quickly, his gaze returning to the watercolor. He tried to study the artwork impartially. It was an impossible task, of course, but even an ignoramus like him could tell that it was good. It was wonderful.

"You're a genius," he said, laying the painting aside and taking Eve in his arms again. "Thank you for understanding how much it would mean to me."

He buried his face in her fragrant hair. The smell of it always reminded him of sunny meadows full of wildflowers. He drew back, meaning to wander around the edge of Eve's face with his mouth, and wondered—

He stopped and lowered his face to her hair again, sniffing. For a minute there, it had reminded him of something burning. The thought barely registered before he pushed her away, jumped up and turned toward the kitchen.

Dark smoke rolled across the ceiling above the stove. He vaulted over the back of the sofa.

"Oh, no!" Eve clapped a hand over her mouth.

By the time she reached the kitchen, Adam had turned off the flame under the chicken. But that wasn't the problem. She stared at the upper oven, one hand again covering her mouth as she remembered the pie.

"Open the window," Adam commanded as he reached for the oven door.

By the time she'd opened the window above the kitchen sink, he was turning with the pie in his mitt-covered hands, surrounded by a cloud of smoke. Dark juice bubbled over the sides of the pie and dripped to the floor. "Put it in the sink," she directed, moving aside.

Black smoke continued to roll out of the oven. She looked from the open oven door to the steaming pie now resting in the sink. The top was dark, but it wasn't burnt. "I don't understand. Where's all the smoke coming from?"

Adam picked up the metal spatula and scraped the bottom of the oven. Black goo covered the shiny metal when he withdrew it. "Juice," he said succinctly, rapping the spatula on the side of the porcelain sink. He returned to the oven and scraped some more.

When he moved toward the sink again, Eve opened the lower oven and removed the now sunken souffle. She set it on the stove and stared at the sad remains of their dinner. A collapsed souffle, too-crisp chicken, mushroom-tarragon sauce that looked like school paste, and a pie singed around the edges.

Adam glanced from the top of the stove to where Eve stood. He leaned over and opened the refrigerator door. "Oh, well, there's always the salad."

A wan smile flitted across her lovely face. He grinned in relief, then heard her chuckle. Closing the refrigerator door, he gathered her to him. "I'm getting you out of here and taking you to dinner." He made sure the stove was off and turned her toward the back door. "Just think what a great story this will make for your children one day."

Eve hurried toward the exit of the thronged mall near Milwaukee. She looked for a fast-food stop since she had to be back in less than an hour so Alice could reach school on time. Spotting one, she stepped out of the stream of people.

Standing in line, she thought again of the discovery she'd just made in the dressing room of a clothing store. With one leg jammed into her pants, preparing to don what she now considered her uniform of jeans, shirt and tennis shoes, she had hesitated. Her matching image teetered in front of her as she balanced on one leg.

Her gaze tracked around the clothes she'd just tried on at the realization she perhaps used protective clothing to make her feel more like she belonged in Adam's world. She constantly had running battles with herself over whether she was being cynical every time she compared her life in Brighton to the one she'd had in Chicago. Making up her mind, she removed the jeans and reached for the hanger of a beautiful, cinnamon-colored silk pants suit.

Straightening her purse strap over the smooth silk, Eve moved up in line to a counter with displays of stuffed croissants. Her wandering gaze followed a bustling waitress in the restaurant that stretched behind the counter, then tracked back at sight of a familiar face. It was the young woman who'd accompanied Jane Hartwig into the store last week. And seated across from her, her back to Eve, was Jane herself no more than twenty feet away.

Eve looked away, inched up in line, and finally gave her order for a ham and cheese croissant and cola. She was waiting for her change when she witnessed a scene that evoked a sense of *déjà vu*. She accepted her change, juggled her packages and escaped.

Driving away, she suddenly knew why the scene in the mall had seemed so familiar. Something similar had happened to her after breaking up with her college sweetheart, and her cheeks still heated when she recalled her own embarrassment as her friend had fled the local canteen. Daphne had been trying to soften the blow of the breakup, but Eve had been too hurt to listen and had shut out her friend.

She eased into the expressway traffic, wondering at the similarities between Jane and herself. Her thoughts went round and round, and she tried to clarify some of them with Alice upon her return.

Explaining about the incident, she said, "Jane still has her mother, of course, but from what Sudie said most of Mrs. Hartwig's time is taken up with running committees. From the little I've seen of Emery Hartwig, he doesn't strike me as the sort to be a pal to his daughter. Rather like the same situation I faced."

Alice's expression softened as she stuffed her briefcase. "It's nice of you to put yourself in Jane's shoes, but you're nothing like her. I don't believe she's ever thought of anyone except herself."

"But don't you see? I *can* sympathize with her, but she's battling on two fronts for attention and receiving very little for her efforts."

A sudden thought made her frown. "There's a tenuous family connection between the Hartwig family and Adam. Maybe that's one of the reasons Jane was drawn to him. Or, maybe that's the way it was in the beginning, and her young heart was captivated by Adam's normal warmth and friendliness. But his dislike of her father and Jane's own persistence in pursuing him has led simply to another person pushing her away."

"I've got to run, but we're going to talk about this later. Promise me."

She nodded as Alice picked up her briefcase, dropped a kiss on her daughter's head and backed away with a wave before she disappeared through the door.

Any thought of Adam brought back memories of her unusual

response to his flirtatious kisses. Karen cooed and waved her arms in excitement.

"Yes, sweetie, I think it's wonderful, too. And before I forget, I'd better call Sudie and talk to her about cooking lessons." Karen jabbered back at her.

"Well, you see, it's simply a matter of swallowing your pride."

Eleven

After almost three weeks of daily rides with Eve, Adam now counted it the highlight of his day. They'd explored the whole surrounding area, but his favorite destination was still the glade overlooking his valley. And he'd made a beeline for it today, feeling territorial as he did.

He watched Eve pack up the remains of an early supper of cold fried chicken he'd sweet-talked Sudie into providing, Eve's pasta salad, as well as some chocolate chip cookies she'd baked. The lessons with his housekeeper must have helped because they'd tasted delicious.

She looked adorable as she scooted around the blanket, her hair coming away in wisps from what she called a French braid, her skin already a warm honey color from their rides. She even had a sprinkling of light freckles across the bridge of her nose.

His heart turned over as she wrinkled that cute little nose at something. Sometime during the last few days, he'd become aware that Eve was as important to him as his ability to heal animals. Thoughts of her colored every aspect of his day. The question of whether a city girl could adapt to country life no longer applied. She had such curiosity and generosity of spirit, she'd probably be as happy as a honeybee in clover wherever she was.

"Come over here," he said, catching one of her hands. With a little tug, she lay practically nose to nose with him. "I promised myself I wouldn't rush things, that I'd give you time. But," his head dipped as he neared her delectable mouth, "I think you should know I have no intention of letting you disappear from my life as easily as you came into it."

Adam saw the impact of his words as Eve's eyes widened. "Why are you so surprised?"

"You—You don't really know anything about me—"

"On the contrary." He cupped her chin, raising her face even closer. "You're lovely, outside and in.

"Everything you've done demonstrates the type of person you are. You tried to be the son your father never had. You learned you didn't like your job so you made up your mind to figure out what you'd like to do. You refused to wallow in self-pity over a broken engagement. More fool he, by the way, but I'm not complaining because his loss is my gain.

"Where were we? Oh. You're empathetic, sympathetic, talented. Give me another week and I'll add to the list. Most important is the fact you're uniquely qualified to fill my dreams."

She still looked stunned so he leaned forward and brushed his lips against hers. He wanted to take her in his arms and convince her of his love, but bit down hard on his desire. *Her* feelings right now were more important than his.

She blinked. "Are you saying you . . . love me?"

"I must not have been doing too good a job of it or you wouldn't be asking."

"But— Don't you think you're being a little hasty?"

"By that you mean *you* think I am." He took a look at the confusion lurking in the depths of her beautiful blue eyes and said, "Why don't you tell me what you're feeling?"

Eve closed her eyes briefly, struggling to overcome the mental wall she'd built over the years. "This isn't easy for me to say, but I think relief is mixed up in there, too. Relief because . . . oh, because I'd sensed a . . . a connection, an attraction, if you will."

"Ah, now we're getting someplace." He grinned. "So you're attracted to me, huh?" He kissed the tip of her nose. "Though I have to tell you that you've done a helluva job disguising it."

"That's because I also wondered about my morals. What kind of person am I to end an engagement and immediately be attracted to another man?"

"I'd stick with relief, if I were you," he said, still grinning. "That little twinge of conscience was nothing more than guilt at being happy when society says you should have been miserable." She had to smile at his logic though she shook her head.

"Look," he said, picking up one of her hands and playing with her fingers, "I did some mental gymnastics and realized the spot you were in." His grin turned sly. "You'll note I was also smart enough to know the attraction was mutual."

"Pretty sure of yourself, aren't you?"

"No, just observant. And very, very hopeful." Adam raised her hand and brushed it against his cheek before his lips touched her knuckles. "If you didn't feel *something*, there was no reason to go riding with me every day. It was either that or you loved my dog and horses."

She smiled at his nonsense, realizing that his ability to make her laugh was one of the things she liked most about him.

"If you want to tell me you love me, too, don't be bashful. Jump in anytime."

The pleasant haze Eve had been enveloped in started to evaporate, and she tensed under his hands. "Oh, Adam. . . ." She knew she liked him tremendously, but love? How could she trust her judgment anymore? The thought brought a frown and she said, "All kidding aside, do you see my dilemma? Everything has happened so quickly. I—I'm not sure of anything right now."

"Don't feel I don't understand," he said, stroking her fingers with his thumb. "Like I said, I'm jumping the gun. I'd meant to wait, give you some time to settle down after that other business, but somehow I just couldn't seem to wait any longer."

That little boy grin stretched beneath his mustache, and she yearned for him to kiss her again.

"My mouth gets me into a lot of trouble."

She could believe it. Any man who kissed as well as he did would find himself in trouble.

"If you don't already know, I have a tendency to say things sometimes before my brain's connected to my mouth."

"Then why don't you quit talking and kiss me?"

"Always happy to oblige a lady." And he did.

Several minutes later she asked on a happy sigh. *"When* did you know?"

A light in her eyes had replaced that dazed look. "If I'm honest, it was probably a lot sooner than I admitted to myself. Probably right after I picked you up when you'd injured your leg. No man gets to be my age without having formed some idea of the type of woman it'd take to make him happy. You're smaller than the mental image I'd fixed on, but believe me, you've got all the essential equipment." He grinned. "And just as important, you've got the heart. Like I said, lovely outside and in."

"I happen to think you're very special too," she said, stretching to meet his lips.

Adam heard the 'but' in her voice and as he'd told her, he *did* understand. So he set about reassuring her. "Let me put it this way. I've got enough confidence for both of us, but I'm not going to rush you to the altar. I'll let you get used to the idea first."

He ran his finger along her bottom lip. It wasn't easy being a gentleman, and he hoped it didn't take her *too* long to realize they belonged together. Meanwhile, there was her lovely mouth.

He was moving too quickly for Eve's peace of mind, but before she could formulate a coherent rebuttal to what he'd said, his lips settled on hers.

Her warm glow returned and grew under his expert touch. *This* was how she'd expected to feel with Richard: taken out of herself so one action followed another naturally. She didn't have to worry which way her mouth slanted under Adam's, she didn't have to wonder if it was too soon to caress his face and touch his lovely mustache with her fingertips. She didn't have to fear she'd hate the feel of his tongue as it slipped through her lips to duel with hers. She didn't have to think about breathing because her body had taken over and done it for her, allowing her to concentrate upon the texture of his lips, his tongue, his mouth.

Adam drew in a shaky breath as he rolled away from Eve and lay with his eyes closed. "I should be shot for taking advantage of you this way, but. . . ." He made a rude sound. "That's twice now. All I can do is promise to try to be a gentleman, but it's not going to be easy."

He concentrated on getting his breathing under control, as well as his aching body. He needed to focus on Eve's feelings. He might know there was no reason for them not to become lovers, but she apparently had some catching up to do mentally. And when she did, he expected incineration if that was an example of—

Her unnatural stillness next to him penetrated his hormonic euphoria. He rolled to his side and looked down at her, at her taut, unhappy expression. "What is it?" he said, reaching for her in concern. "What's wrong?"

"You don't have to pretend just to spare my feelings." Wasn't that always the way it worked for her? Just when she thought she had the brass ring, reality intruded. "I assure you I'm used to this reaction."

She tried to rise, but Adam simply leaned further over and pinned her to the blanket. He stared at her and shook his head. "I don't understand. I must've missed something."

A crushing weight filled Eve's chest. But it wasn't the dear feel of his body next to hers; only the disappointment that another man had found her lacking. As in the past, pride came to her rescue, and she fought the quick flash of embarrassment warming her by staring into his eyes.

"I know my . . . physical response leaves a lot to be desired." His expression slipped farther into bewilderment, and she became angry. "Two men have already told me that so—"

"Whoa!"

Suddenly, she found herself sitting upright and staring into blank astonishment. After a moment, Adam's hands relaxed. His fingers slid up to cup her shoulders at the same moment a grin returned under his damned sexy mustache. She wanted to smack him!

"Honey, someone's been pulling your leg. I can assure you there's nothing wrong with your response." His grin split into a full-blown smile. "In fact, the *only* reason I backed off was because I was enjoying it a little too much."

Eve would have pushed him away then if she could have, even though she wanted to believe him. But he had continued to slip his hands over her shoulders until his arms pinned her against him. "If you like," he said, his lips almost upon hers, "I'd be more than happy to give you another demonstration." He didn't wait for permission.

She resisted the pressure of his mouth for a few moments, but his hands at her back urged her closer. Without knowing how, she found herself on her knees with his body imprinting itself on hers. His hands drifted lower, cupping her bottom and raising her until the apex of their thighs met. With his hard body pressed against her, she could no longer doubt his sincerity—or the proof of his words. She melted against him with a sigh.

Her surrender was so sweet and his need to reassure her so great that it was several minutes before Adam could bring himself to ease his embrace. His mouth continued to trace a trail of light kisses along the delicate skin of Eve's throat. But when he found his lips questing farther south, he pulled her head to his chest and rested his chin on top of her fragrant curls.

"If that doesn't prove anything to you," he said unsteadily, "then I think it fair to warn you the next attempt will bare more than my soul."

Through the thudding of Adam's heart next to her ear, Eve heard his words and smiled. Her blood raced as fast and warm as his, but the knowledge she could affect him so also calmed her. And while his words conjured visions of titillating excitement, they also tickled her.

She pulled back with a little laugh. "What, before God and everyone?"

He smiled down at her. "I don't think God would mind, but if it bothers you that much I'll send Sheba home and blindfold the horses."

Linking his hands behind her, he leaned away and surveyed her as she giggled like a young girl. Laughter was good for her. And healing. His little City Girl had been too solemn when he first met her.

"I'm glad you can see things in a truer perspective and laugh about it. But what other idiot besides your ex-fiancé was fool enough not to realize what a treasure he had?"

She twined her arms about his neck and pulled his head toward her. The same leap of excitement was there as their lips met, but instead of demanding, he kept his touch reassuring.

As his mouth settled on hers, Eve felt the flutter of desire before his lips gentled hers into acceptance. She'd never before realized the language of a kiss could be so evocative. She already knew she could raise a firestorm between them. But she now learned that besides encouragement of their mutual joy, there was also the warmth of comfort, as well as an inspiration for faith in him, and the promise of love.

This time when his lips withdrew, she kept her eyes closed and remained still, savoring the experience. "Oh, my. You do that so very well."

"I'd like to remind you I didn't do it alone." Adam gathered her close, next to his heart. "And I think that's my point. It takes two to tango, as they say. Why would you let someone tell you the blame was yours?"

"I'm only now beginning to realize that it wasn't." Eve withdrew from his arms and settled next to him on the blanket. "I had never been seriously involved with anyone until my last year at college. Most of the feeling turned out to be on my side, since he let me know my tepid responses didn't warrant any great displays on his part. I learned rather painfully that he was more interested in what my father and uncle could do for him in a business sense."

Peeking at Adam, she saw his brows had furrowed, but he didn't interrupt or offer false platitudes, for which she was grateful. But she also realized with her newfound knowledge that remembering the experience didn't pain her as much. Gnawing guilt about her poor showing as a woman had been alleviated, and only sadness remained for the girl who'd lacked so much confidence.

"That experience, unfortunately, only deepened my impression of not having very much to offer someone. Looking back, I can see my anxiety only made me become more inhibited as I grew older."

Adam enfolded her hands in his, raising them to his lips. "Reserved, yes. Inhibited, no." He kissed her hands again and said, "Go on."

"Richard more or less snuck in through the back door." At his questioning look, she explained, "He was a protégé of my father's and I was used to his being around. When my father died, Richard pulled me through most of the trauma. We spent so much time together that when he raised the question of marriage, it seemed almost a natural extension of our lives. I was comfortable with him, I trusted him. . . ."

She wrinkled her nose and made a face. "A mistake, of course. But even before I realized that, I'd begun to have second thoughts. Richard wasn't so patient any longer with my . . . reserved, I believe is the word you used . . . my reserved attitude. The more he pushed, the more panicked I became."

When she sat quietly, her hands linked with his, Adam probed gently. "So, you gave him his marching orders?"

A little sigh escaped her. "Unfortunately, no. Before I could work up the courage to break things off, I discovered his interest in me pretty much paralleled my college sweetheart's."

Eve's rueful expression told Adam more than words that her healing process had already begun. But if he ever came within a yard of Richard, he'd pay the man back for hurting Eve in coin the idiot could understand.

She looked at him uncertainly. "Do you want to know the sordid details?"

"No," he declared, taking her in his arms once more. "It makes my blood pressure rise to even *think* of how he must have hurt you."

Eve didn't tell him that his ardent soothing was unnecessary; she enjoyed it too much to protest. She was surprised to find he looked serious when at last he pulled away. "I got the idea when I met your uncle a few weeks ago that he's pretty well off. What you've said only reinforces that impression. But I want you to know you have nothing to worry about financially. It won't be anything fancy, but between the farm and the clinic, I can provide a comfortable life for us.

"Just understand I love you, *you* with your splendid heart and wonderful talent, whether your uncle comes through or not."

"Oh, Adam—" His words touched her so deeply that his image wavered through sudden tears. *Now* was the time to tell him all about the real Eve, and she meant to. She swore she did. But he kissed her tears away and said they'd talk later; they had to take advantage of Sheba being off on a romp. And soon she lost the ability to think at all.

There was a lot to be said for concentrating on the mundane, Eve decided as she tumbled into bed that night in a fog of exhaustion. It kept the mind too busy to ponder personal problems.

But now that there was nothing to distract her—no meal to prepare or dishes to wash, no slightly shrunken discolored clothes to put away, no canvas to be painted nor brushes to clean, no Adam to kiss her senseless—she couldn't escape her thoughts.

Happiness filled her as memories of the day rushed back, and she spent many minutes lost in a glorious reverie. And yet . . . yet it wasn't unclouded joy. A sliver of fear remained from other painful memories. As much as she wanted to believe she could build a new life in Wisconsin, she was realistic enough to realize there were problems.

Sure she was enthralled now by the people here and the seemingly simpler lifestyle. But would that wear off in a matter of weeks or months? Was she talented enough to make painting her life's work or was she kidding herself? And most important of all, how would Adam react when she told him about the real Eve Sutton?

She'd felt nothing but relief this evening when Adam had left still uninformed because of yet another emergency. She'd wanted to hug to herself a little longer the undiluted specialness of the day. But she owed Adam the truth. She told herself she'd find another moment to tell him. Soon.

Twelve

Eve patted the couch cushion again, then gave it up. Everything had already been cleaned, straightened and restraightened. Twice. Adam was due any minute to help her finish putting the dinner together she'd started earlier with Sudie.

In inspiration, she fetched the chilled bottle of blush wine and opened it. She poured two glasses, still searching for a way to give Adam full disclosure, as she thought of her background.

But when he opened the screen door a few minutes later, she had yet to find the perfect words.

He stepped behind her and nuzzled her neck. "Hmmmm, my favorite flavor."

"What, me or the wine?"

"Silly girl." He nipped the side of her neck. "You notice I didn't attack that wine first."

After turning in his arms and greeting him properly, she handed him a glass, picked up her own and led the way to the sofa. "We'll get started in a few minutes. First, I want—"

"First," he interrupted, "a toast." He held his glass next to hers. "What shall we make it?"

"To new beginnings." Her throat was tight, and she could barely swallow the sip she forced herself to take. Setting down her glass, she said, "That was more appropriate than you know."

"Hey." He set down his own glass and cupped her cheek. "Why so serious? I thought I'd convinced you dinner was no problem. *I'm* not a picky eater nor," he added with a grin, "am I afraid to be a guinea pig."

Eve tried to smile. "It's not the dinner." His big hand felt so warm and comforting. She drew strength from it and covered it with one of hers. "It's about us. Or about me, actually."

His smile slipped and he watched her warily. Good lord, this was harder than she'd thought. Rushing her words, she said, "I didn't get a chance to explain yesterday, but I didn't want you to get the wrong idea. Or rather, I think you have the wrong idea and I want to straighten things out."

Her hand over his tensed as her few carefully prepared words fled from her mind. She hurried into speech at his fierce expression. "You see, I—I own a small electronics firm, or rather my family does. I know how you feel about people like Hartwig, and I didn't want you to think my uncle and I are anything like him. I—"

"Good lord!" Adam tightened his grasp and tilted Eve's face for a quick, hard kiss. "As if I'd think you were anything like him." He shook her chin gently. "Don't ever scare me like that again. I thought you were going to tell me you'd changed your mind about staying in Brighton, that you were going back to Chicago."

Her worried expression melted into one of concern as she caressed his face. "Oh, no."

He didn't give her a chance to say more, but crushed her to him as his lips covered hers. The thunder of his heart at the scare she had given him slowed. In the quiet of their kiss, he heard Sheba whining and drew back reluctantly rather than have her attacking them at this moment.

Though her eyes looked dazed and her lovely mouth damp from his kiss, Eve still wore a faintly anxious air. "You don't mind then?"

"No," he said, wrapping his arms around her and pulling her head to his chest. "I told you. If your uncle wants to give you some money, that's his perogative. But it has nothing to do with us. Spend the money on yourself, give it away, I don't care which."

With Adam's arms wrapped about her, his hands reached around her sides. His fingers brushed against her breasts, and they tingled, causing tension to spiral through her. The hard muscles of his arms flexed under her fingers, and she turned her face to kiss his chest through his shirt. She dragged her eyes open, meaning to inch her way up to reach his neck—and saw Sheba's head resting on the sofa cushion next to them, watching her intently.

"Don't look now," Eve said, trying to ease their embrace, "but we have company."

Adam's hands slid tantalizingly across her body as he slewed around. He groaned and dropped his head to her shoulder. "Not again."

"Yes, again," she said on a ripple of laughter. "We'll have several interesting stories to tell *our* children."

Two days later, Eve's fingers fumbled the bridle bit as she raced to saddle the nervous horse. Treasure snorted and tossed her head, so she had to stop and calm the mare before trying again. She wondered what on earth had happened to Adam to cause such an uproar.

She hadn't been home from her cooking lesson with Sudie ten minutes when the phone rang, with Adam's housekeeper on the other end. The unflappable Sudie had been so upset that it'd taken Eve several minutes to untangle what she said. Martha Diehl had called Sudie because Adam had not returned to the clinic like he'd said he would after visiting Emery at the bank. Instead, she'd seen him "roar by in his truck looking madder than a hornet."

Sudie had kept an eye out for him. And sure enough, he'd "zoomed by the house just a few minutes ago like the devil himself was after him." Emery plus Adam equaled trouble with a capital 'T.' Since he wasn't with Eve and he hadn't come home, it meant he'd decided to ride out his anger. Would Eve go after him to make sure he didn't break his fool neck?

Adam's truck was parked in front of the barn, but he'd already left by the time Eve reached it. Her trepidation increased when she found his saddle resting beside hers. He'd ridden bareback, which only confirmed Sudie's suspicion that something was seriously wrong.

With Treasure saddled, Eve, still wearing one of her new silk pants suits, mounted her. She thought she knew where Adam would wind up; she only hoped she was right.

She never caught sight of him as she threaded her way through orchards and around cultivated fields before heading for the far end of the valley. Finally, she turned Treasure's head toward the hill and they started climbing. The silk proved slippery but, clenching with her knees, Eve hung onto the pommel with one hand. At last she heard the ripple of water and turned the horse to follow it upstream.

Her heart crashed against her ribs when she spotted the meadow and found it empty. Then a horse snickered from the trees, and Treasure made a beeline for her stablemate. Lucky had been staked to graze, but where was Adam? Eve tied her horse on a loose rein and remembered the family cemetery.

She saw him as she came through the trees, hunkered down on his heels by Ramsey's headstone. He projected a figure of defeat with his shoulders slumped, his head hanging down. She stopped at the wrought-iron gate, unsure now if she should interrupt his solitude. But his obvious unhappiness tugged at her heart. Even if he turned her away, she had to try to help him.

She slipped through the open gate and made her way silently to his side. "Adam?"

He didn't answer, but after a moment he held a hand out to her. Grasping it, she knelt in the grass. A brief glance at his bowed head under the Stetson revealed a face wracked by grief, so she studied Ramsey's headstone to grant him some privacy.

The newest and the largest headstone in the family plot, the marble marker towered over them. Eve couldn't help a smile as she read the engraved words again:

"Not a pharaoh, not a prince or a pauper,
But a good man and father, and a great granddad."

Adam shifted next to her as he raised his head and regarded the tombstone. "His dream is dead. But as God is my witness, I don't think even he would've wanted me to reunite the valley under Emery's terms."

"What's happened?"

"Emery made me an offer he thought I couldn't refuse—a trade for the land I've always wanted back. In return, he'd announce my engagement to his daughter Jane." Adam didn't appear to hear her sharply drawn breath of surprise. "Jane has my complete sympathy right now. She's a spoiled brat, but she doesn't deserve this. I told Emery if I ever heard a whisper of his proposal around town, I'd come after him with a horsewhip."

He sighed wearily. "I feel I've let Granddad down, but I don't see what else I could've done."

Eve's heart went out to him at the anguish on his face and for what he must be feeling. He'd had the courage to give up a life-long dream. Did she? She measured her heart and swallowed, but the self-sacrificing words wouldn't come. Miserable, she said, "I wish I could tell you to go ahead and do what you have to. But I can't. I'm not so noble I can just give you up."

He gave her a smile of heartbreaking sweetness. "Thank God," he said, his voice husky, "because you mean more to me than this valley does."

She threw her arms around his neck. "Oh, Adam."

Knocked off balance, he rolled back, bringing Eve down on top of him. Her face hung above his for a moment, her hair lit to a dazzling glow by a shaft of sunlight, her blue eyes gleaming with unshed tears. Emery could keep the land; with Eve by his side, *he* was the richest man in the world. Why had it taken him so long to realize his feelings for this City Girl were more than simple lust? He loved her so much it hurt. Threading his fingers through strands of gold, he brought her mouth down to his and drowned in her sweetness.

Her pliancy against the hard planes of his body ignited his desire. Leaving the tangle of her hair, his hands roamed over the curves of her hips and derriere, the softness of her clothes aiding him in his discovery.

He turned to his side when he felt his blood heating out of control. With his lips, he traced the delicate vein at her temple.

"So soft," he said, then realized the material under his hands resembled her skin. Pulling back, he took a good look at her. He gave a silent whistle at the picture she made, soft brown and golds on the bed of green. All the while his hand stroked the texture of the fabric on her hip, feeling the heat of her firm young body. "What is this? It feels almost as soft as you do."

"Sueded silk."

"Silk, huh?" He grinned. "I think my fantasies just received a new outlook." Before they had a chance to cut loose, he rose. "Come on, I just realized we don't have our chaperone with us, and you're lethal in that outfit."

Retrieving his hat, he settled it on his head with one last look at his granddad's grave. In spite of the way things had turned out, he knew Ramsey would have approved. That was all that mattered.

Adam led her back to the meadow where they settled side by side in a patch of sun-splashed clover. He removed his Stetson and passed her the remains of their last picnic bottle of wine. "Sorry, no glasses."

After taking a drink himself, he dangled the bottle from a hand resting on an upraised knee. Eve leaned against him, and he put his other arm around her shoulder as they both stared down the length of his valley. Their love was so new that Adam's declaration still seemed a surprise. But the real surprise was the fact they'd both apparently wrapped their true feelings inside enough words to protect themselves until such time as they could absorb the truth. She'd never been so introspective before coming here, never having had the time nor the inclination. The people and the place were changing her, or she was changing because of them. The lowering sun cast shadows across the undulating land, creating new variations of colors. It was the same place, yet different than it had been the last time she'd seen it.

Thoughts about the land reminded her of Adam's loss as his fingers idly traced a pattern on her upper arm, the warmth of his hand fanning the embers of her recent arousal. To distract both of them, she said, "By chaperone, did you mean Sheba?"

"Right the first time." He looked down at her with a grin. "I ever tell you how smart you are for a city girl?"

"Oh, I'm smart all right. Smart enough to be president of the family business. But it wasn't until I came here that I used that intelligence to smarten up."

He pulled her even closer. "Madame president, huh?"

She snuggled against him, as secure in his love as she was in the knowledge she'd made the right decision to trust again. It hadn't been easy, but it was proving worthwhile.

"My father was wrong. He insisted the way to run things was to maintain your distance, yet I always felt isolated, lonely doing it his way. I must be a people person because I've discovered a great deal of joy here simply by being myself and getting involved with people."

"No wonder you were so unhappy before." His lips trailed up the side of her neck to her temple, making her shiver. "Remember I told you you were made for sunshine and laughter? It's better when it's shared. I'm just glad you picked me to share it with."

"As I remember, it was you who did the picking."

"We can spend the next fifty years arguing about it." His mouth moved along her jawline.

She turned her head toward his seeking lips, then turned about in his arms. The now-familiar warmth bloomed inside as he pulled her to him and reclined in the grass and clover.

Adam felt the drift from sweet surrender into passion, but when he would have eased away, she linked her hands behind his neck.

"No chaperone, remember? I think this is the perfect time to have a good, old-fashioned necking session."

His pulse jumped, but he ruthlessly strangled his rising passion. "To a point. But I have to tell you," he said with a grin, "that I rather like the idea of an old-fashioned wedding night." He chuckled at the deepening bloom on Eve's skin. "Besides, your uncle more or less entrusted you to my care, and I feel honor bound to protect you—even from myself."

The flush riding her cheeks deepened, but Eve's gaze held his. Her beautiful Madonna smile appeared as her hands played with the hair on his neck. "Correct me if I'm wrong, but you did say your intentions were honorable."

"You better believe it, City Girl." His voice was rough as he added, "But the key word there is 'honorable.' "

"Whatever you say, Adam."

Her absolute trust left him shaken as their lips met. His naive little love might be a woman, but she was as innocent as the day she'd been born. His desire flamed anew even as he determined to put his needs aside and focus on her. Just Eve and what would please her.

His gentle hands became instruments of torture as they stroked over Eve, building the flame of warmth inside until she writhed. Closer, she wanted to be closer. Her mouth slid down his neck to the hollow at the base of his throat, and she felt as well as heard his groan.

Adam stilled as her hands played over his chest, molding to the sweep and hollow of the muscles he held under rigid control as her lips followed.

"My turn," he said, tracing a hand lovingly across the front of her blouse and the softness of sueded silk covering silky skin. He moved it aside only to discover another scrap of silkiness underneath as he worshipped her body and told her how beautiful she was.

Eve inhaled raggedly as his lips skimmed the edge of the silk separating them, tantalizing touches of his mouth igniting tiny explosions along unknown nerve endings. She arched under him as his mouth found a nipple and lost her breath at the exquisite pull from the center of her being, a quickening response that only Adam had ever been able to raise within her. She was so lucky to have found him.

Regretfully, Adam left the tantalizing taste of her skin and eased his body a hairsbreadth away. She lay beautifully flushed from his loving. "Lordy, sugar, I'm about to go off like a Fourth of July rocket."

When she'd caught her breath, Eve opened her eyes. They lay at the edge of the sun-dappled meadow, the scent of crushed clover surrounding them. Gradually bird song and the rustling of leaves replaced the roaring in her ears.

She ran her hands possessively over Adam's powerful shoulders and said next to his ear, "Your valley is our own Garden of Eden."

Eve paced the kitchen, willing the telephone to ring. When she'd spoken to her uncle last night, he'd promised to call back early this morning. She had to try to do something about the land

Emery Hartwig held. To withhold it from Adam as he planned was simply wicked.

She looked doubtfully at the phone. She had a number of calls to make about their fledgling foundation, but didn't want to tie up the line. It proved difficult to concentrate since her mind kept wandering to the interlude with Adam in the meadow. Even the memory of the sensations he aroused made her feel giddy.

When the phone rang moments later, she snatched up the receiver. "Hello?"

Her uncle chuckled. "Relax, all is well. I found a Wisconsin attorney to handle the purchase. I've instructed him to call the local real estate office, then the bank, searching for suitable 'farm land.' "

"Who did you decide to use for the purchaser?"

"Since you didn't want our name to appear, Simms will front for us. But Hartwig will never see him. I'm forwarding his power of attorney to the lawyer, who will handle all the paperwork."

"Thank you, Uncle Robb."

"My pleasure. I'll let you know when everything is signed so the title can be transferred to you. Then I'll express the papers for final signature."

"That's great, except I want ownership of the property transferred to Adam Wagner."

"Adam, huh? Is there anything else going on I should know about?"

"Not yet, Uncle Robb. I want to give the deed to Adam on his birthday a little over a week from now. Do you think that will be a problem?"

"Shouldn't be, but I'll let you know if so. By the way, any idea what you want to call this foundation we're setting up?"

With the thought of Adam and his valley constantly in the back of her mind, she replied, "Eden. The Eden Foundation."

"Sounds good to me. Send me the business plans and other particulars like we discussed, and we're in business."

Eve thanked him again and hung up. The Eden Foundation. That was as close as she could come to the fairy godmother Adam had mentioned as being necessary. She hoped it would be enough.

Hearing an engine, she looked out the kitchen window. Adam had just pulled up in his truck. She went to the door and watched him approach, full of pride at his long, rangy stride. When he saw her through the screen, his eyes lit up and a grin split beneath his mustache.

"Hello, beautiful."

He opened the door and pulled her into his embrace in one fluid motion, lifting her off the floor. As the warmth of his arms closed around her, she felt cherished and safe. But the safety she felt with Adam was different from the safety she'd felt with her choice of Richard as a mate. Then, no real emotion had been involved; it was the practical thing to do. Now, just the thought of Adam caused her insides to soften, and she knew true happiness would only be hers with this man. She tilted her head back and, as her cheek slid by his searching for his mouth, absorbed his fresh scent of soap and aftershave.

Having become immediately aroused at the sight of Eve standing there with her legs showcased in shorts, Adam gloried in her response. He wondered again at his luck in finding someone so sweet, talented and sexy all rolled into one. The pressure inside his jeans increased, and he cursed the remaining calls to be made. He withdrew from the honey taste of her mouth and slid his lips to one of his favorite places, her temple.

"Hmmm. I like the way you say good morning."

Her fingernails tantalized his neck before her fingers dived into the hair curling over his collar. His pulse lept in response but remembering the calls, he forced himself to let her slide to the floor as she said, "You smell like you just stepped out of the shower."

"I did. My last call was a messy one, and I couldn't stand myself." Since the weather had turned warm, she wore a sleeveless blouse and he couldn't resist the temptation of running his hands over the silky smoothness of her skin. "Before I get distracted again, I did have a purpose in coming here."

"You mean other than kissing me good morning?"

"As enjoyable as that is, yes." He kissed her again, lightly in self-protection. "I have a high school student who comes in every day to help, only she's hitting the books for finals. Do you think you could lend a hand now and then when you finish at Alice's?"

"Sure, but what would I be doing?" She looped her arms around his waist and leaned back so she could look up at him.

He enjoyed seeing her beautifully expressive face, but her body pressed against a sensitive part of his anatomy played hell with his libido. "You could handle the phones and incoming appointments. That would help a lot."

"Sure. Would you mind if I used your typewriter or computer, whatever it is, while I'm there?"

He shook his head, enjoying the way her smile lit up her face. "No, why?"

"Oh, just some marketing information I need to pull together for an idea a group of us is working on."

"I won't be able to come back this morning for a ride. Too busy. Besides, it's getting hot outside. Maybe we could go for a swim after finishing at the clinic. Sound good?"

"Ummm, wonderful." She stretched and touched her lips to his.

He thought the idea great too, especially when he remembered she'd be wearing a bathing suit that exposed even more of her tempting body.

News spread that Emery Hartwig had put the property he held in the valley on the market without giving Adam a chance at it. When word later passed around that it'd been sold, feelings ran high against him. Eve worried that Jane would be regarded in the same light as her father, but didn't know what she could do about it.

Her life had become so full and she so busy, she barely had time to think. Her expertise as a portrait artist, in pencil sketches, watercolor or oil, became a "nine day wonder," according to Sudie. Especially when people saw the work she'd done with Sheba and a few of the children's pets at the clinic. Suddenly, she was flooded with requests to do animals, as well as children and some adults.

"What are you going to charge?" Alice asked in amusement as Eve fretted about finding time to do everything.

"I hadn't really thought about it."

She'd given the sketches of animals at the clinic to the children as a way to distract them from their pets' problems. And she'd found her shelves filling with jars of canned fruit, vegetables, and honey as thanks.

"I don't know," she said again. "I guess I'll charge a few dollars for the sketches and a little more for the watercolors and oils. Enough to keep me in supplies."

"You can't do that."

Eve looked up from the mat she was working on at the tone of Alice's voice. "Why, what's wrong?"

"In the first place, if you practically give your artwork away, people won't value it. And at the bargain basement prices you're thinking of, you'll be inundated with commissions. You'll have even less time to yourself."

"But I don't need the money."

Looking both exasperated and amused at the same time, Alice planted her hands on her hips. "You might not, but what about the other artists I represent?" she said, throwing a hand toward the front of the store. "How do you think it's going to affect their sales if you give your artwork away?"

"Oh, good grief. All I want to do is paint, not turn it into a business."

Alice grinned. "I've got a simple solution. Appoint me your agent and leave it in my hands."

Eve did so gladly. The response to their canvas of possible business interest had been overwhelming. She had quickly put Sudie in charge of coordinating all their efforts since she had enough to handle with the store, the clinic, finding time to paint, let alone time to spend with Adam, as she firmed up marketing plans. Their meeting had been moved up because of all the interest generated.

Learning about some of the business ideas over lunch that day, she made a mental note to call her uncle. This was getting to be more than they could handle on their own. They decided to bring someone in from the real estate office to help find space for everyone and to combine some of the smaller businesses into shared office space.

"Good idea," Sudie said. "Now how about lending some of that sense to plans for Adam's birthday party? We haven't settled any of the details, just talked about it. Time's getting short."

"It's a week from this Friday, isn't it?" Sudie nodded as Eve realized the date originally had been the one when she'd planned to leave the cabin to return home. So much had happened in such a short time. "Okay, how many people do you plan to invite?"

Sudie glanced up at the ceiling as she did some mental arithmetic. "Oh, about a hundred or so."

"One hundred!" Eve stared at her. "I thought you meant a couple dozen people. No wonder you're starting to push the panic button."

"With Adam born and raised here, there are a lot of people whose nose would be out of joint if we didn't invite them." Alice, Clarel and Connie all nodded in agreement. "In fact, we probably should plan on at least fifty more to be safe."

Eve insisted on handling the party arrangements since she was staying rent-free at Adam's. Their eyes widened at her mention of a caterer, tents, a band, dance floor, lighting, servers and bartenders. They agreed it was necessary though because of having to organize the foundation meetings, too.

Eve exhaled in relief. Just when she thought she really belonged here, she'd had to stick her big city foot in her mouth. She should have known she wouldn't get off so lightly though. Pushing Karen in her stroller back to the store, she caught Alice looking at her a few times. Finally her friend said, "It's none of my business, of course, but I wondered how you know so much about these foundation requirements and catered affairs."

She didn't mind explaining her family wealth to Adam, but she'd been careful to avoid any hint of it to others, especially since she didn't want any connection between her and the Eden Foundation. But some details were bound to come out eventually; maybe it was time to lay some of the groundwork.

Without consciously doing so, she chose almost the same words she'd used with Adam to explain her family-owned business. "I've organized the Christmas parties and annual picnics for years."

"So that's where you picked up the experience in marketing you mentioned?"

"Yes. In fact, I'm president." As Alice blinked at her news, she added, "But not for long, hopefully. My uncle and I are trying to arrange an employee buy out."

"Well, thank goodness for that. I was beginning to worry you and Adam would have to have a long-distance relationship."

Eve smiled at her relief and, as Alice unlocked the door, said, "By the way, I don't mind if you mention my being president to the others. You know, Sudie, Clarel and Connie. I just didn't want to make a big deal about it."

Alice made a face at her. "As if you'd make a big deal about anything."

A few days later, Eve stared at Adam in consternation and wished he had a little of her reticence. Even Alice had given her some static about accepting a commission for an oil painting of Emery Hartwig's thoroughbred Wind Dancer. But Adam had become almost apoplectic.

"But I'm not sure you understand," she said, trying to see his expression as he stubbornly faced away from her.

Summer seemed to be truly under way at last, and they'd taken to riding early in the mornings when he didn't have emergency calls. Since it was so warm, they'd walked the horses on the return trip to cool them down so they could drink at the lake.

Not knowing what else to do, Eve stepped in front of Adam, even if it did mean she had to stand in two inches of water. "I'm not doing the painting for Emery Hartwig himself. Jane asked me to do it as a gift from her to her father. I'm doing it for Jane," she repeated since his expression hadn't changed from lowered brows and a grim line under his mustache. Finally, she laid a hand on his folded arms. "Did you hear me?"

He glared down at her. "What difference does it make who you're doing it for? The end result is the same."

Eve lowered her head against his arm. How could such a normally reasonable man be so unreasonable on the subject of Emery Hartwig? Then she sighed, knowing the answer very well. He'd suffered a great deal at the hands of Jane's father, maybe even had his grandfather's life shortened some years because of Emery's intransigence. How could she make him understand her feelings of sharing a bond with Jane?

"Adam, you said yourself that you felt sorry for Jane, and—"

"Yes, but I didn't fawn all over her to make her feel better either."

"I'm not fawning over her," Eve said sharply, withdrawing her hand from his arm. Realizing it wouldn't solve anything for them both to lose their tempers, she took a deep breath. "Look, maybe I can explain it to you this way." She told him about the similarities in her and Jane's lives. "I feel this is an opportunity to make a connection with her. Perhaps the last chance we'll have before she becomes as implacable and unfeeling as her father."

"She already is. You just don't realize it yet." He tugged on the reins and led Lucky away from the water. Pulling the leather straps over the stallion's head, he looked back where she still stood in the water. "You do what you want. Just don't expect me to like it." With that he mounted and cantered away.

Eve stared after him in disbelief. Giving in to her desire to kick something, she sliced at the water with her wet boot.

Thirteen

Since Adam had been the one to walk away from their argument, Eve waited with interest to see if his temper had cooled by the time she walked into the clinic that afternoon. When she found Adam and Martha, they were bent over a cat on the examining table.

"Hi," she said, leaning in the doorway. "Just letting you know I've arrived."

Instead of his usual greeting of "Hello, beautiful," Adam ignored her. Sensing something wrong, Martha looked from him to her with a frown. Apparently he was still angry. She smiled at Martha and closed the door.

Giving him a wide berth, Eve remained at the desk answering calls and tailoring some marketing ideas for specific businesses. Their meeting had been a huge success, thanks to her uncle taking her advice and hiring the female attorney Connie had recommended for the foundation. The lawyer in turn had told Sudie that the foundation wanted to hire her to continue in the same capacity as coordinator. It was a stroke of genius because Sudie knew everything about everyone, even new residents, and would be likely to know candidates' weaknesses. She could remain part-time until she tired of it or it became too much to handle on a part-time basis. Then Sudie would have to decide if she wanted to do it full-time. Remembering that, Eve sighed. In his present mood, Adam might blame her if he lost his housekeeper.

Martha tiptoed out at closing time and whispered, "Is something wrong between you and Adam?"

Eve picked up her purse and papers and surprised herself by replying sunnily, "Nothing but a lover's quarrel. It'll blow over."

She hoped. But driving out to Hartwig Farms, she made up her mind she was doing the right thing. If she struck out, so be it; at least she'd have tried. Having decided that Adam had given up on Jane too easily, she'd also made up her mind not to let him sway her. She was through placating men. If she and Adam were to have a successful relationship, she had to be able to do what she thought right. Just like he would expect to do.

But Adam was waiting for her when she returned home that evening. When he'd kissed her thoroughly, he murmured words of apology. "I told you my mouth gets me into trouble. Anything to do with Emery raises a red flag and seems to disconnect my brain. My mouth flaps and words pour out. I don't remember half what I said this morning. I love you and I'm sorry. Say you forgive me, idiot that I am."

They managed to completely surprise Adam with the party on his birthday. Stunned, he looked down into Eve's sparkling eyes and wide smile. Picking her up, he spun her in a circle before kissing her. Overcome, all he could say was, "Thank you," before being engulfed by his friends.

Several hours later, Adam tugged Eve after him and wove among noisy tables to the dance floor. Waiters, flowers, and the glitter of fairy lights attached to tent poles still made him smile as he pulled her into his arms.

"When you surprise someone, you really do a bang-up job."

"I wanted to make it special for you."

He lowered his head and brushed her ear with his lips. "You're special, and that's enough for me."

The look she gave him made him wish everyone else would suddenly disappear. He thought again of the ring tucked away in his jacket pocket that he'd planned to give her at dinner, tempted to do it now. Then someone bumped into them, and he let the idea go. This jumble of friends was too public; he'd wait until he could do it privately.

Though she was having fun, the evening was long for Eve, too. People started leaving around midnight, but it was after one before the bartenders and waitresses cleared away the last of the party debris.

She had long since removed her high heels, and the tapered hem of her silk skirt almost dragged on the dew-laden grass as she and Adam crossed the lawn to the house.

He closed and locked the door. "At last." He loosened his tie and shrugged out of his suit jacket, pulling her toward the fireplace. He dropped onto a sofa, and she sank into his lap. It felt so good to sit down. Too much wine and champagne, too much dancing in heels she'd grown unaccustomed to wearing. "Now I have a surprise for *you,*" he whispered, nuzzling her temple.

"Oh, good. I love surprises."

He sat back, holding a diamond solitaire ring between his fingers. "The month is up, but I don't want you to think I'm trying to rush you. It's just that I thought the timing was right."

"Oh, Adam. It's lovely."

She held out her left hand so he could put the ring on her finger. She gazed at it, filled with love for the man responsible for her being able to turn her life around. She flung her arms around him.

"I take it that means you'll marry me?"

"Most definitely," she managed to say before his lips captured her. When he finally loosened his arms, she remembered her own surprise. "My turn," she said, pulling out of his embrace to open the drawer of the coffee table. She put an over-size, long envelope into his hands. "The oil painting filled the bill when everyone gave you gifts this evening, but this is your real birthday present."

"I've already got the best present any man could want. You."

She pushed at the envelope. "Open."

He tore it apart and fumbled with the long sheets inside. He grinned at her as he managed to unfold and smooth them out. She watched him blink a couple of times to focus on the type-written pages. His face began to tighten as he took in the words.

By the time he'd reached the bottom of the page, a scowl had long since replaced Adam's usual smile.

"What the hell is this?" he said, sitting up straight.

But by then, Eve had already seen the pit yawning at her feet. She stood up, stammering, "It—It's the deed to the property. The two parcels Emery Hartwig held."

"I know *that*," he bit off as he stood to face her. "What I want to know is how you got it and why my name's on it."

She shifted from one foot to the other, miserably aware he'd taken her offering in the wrong way.

"I—I bought it through a third party, so he wouldn't know the purchase was for you." She rubbed her forehead with a shaking hand. "I don't understand. It's a gift from me to you. Why are you so angry, Adam?"

If possible, the thin line of his mouth tightened even more. He dropped the papers. Sheets skittered in several directions to the floor as he slid the knot of his tie back into position.

"If you're that obtuse, then I guess I'll have to spell it out for you. I threw Emery's offer back in his teeth. What am I supposed to do with yours?"

"But he was trying to bribe you. This is a gift!"

"You want to explain the difference? The result is the same. They both emasculate me!"

She gasped as first the venom, then the meaning, of his words sank in. She shook her head, trying to clear away the fog surrounding her, trying to make sense of the misunderstanding. Then she had to close her eyes and grope for the sofa as dizziness struck. When she'd lowered herself to the cushion, she opened her eyes with a streak of pain, only his expression hadn't changed from one of intense dislike, almost—she shuddered—of hatred.

"I can see you're having trouble understanding that. Even when you knew how I felt about Hartwig, you *still* did it."

"But this isn't about you and Hartwig. It's about us. He doesn't come into it."

"I'd like to know how you figure that when the property was in his name to start with. What did you do," he asked, bending over the coffee table, "borrow the money from your uncle to pull this off? That's just great! You beggar yourself to take my manhood away." He flung back to the fireplace and braced his hands against the fieldstone wall.

Eve placed both feet level with the floor, but it didn't help the spinning sensation in her head. "Wait, I don't understand. Why would I have to borrow money from my uncle?"

"How else did you get it?"

"But I told you. We own—"

"Yeah, I know. A small electronics firm." He glared at her. "You drive a secondhand car, your uncle has to buy you a fancy coffee maker, and you expect me to believe you could come up with the cash to buy out Hartwig? Don't make me laugh."

"Coffee maker?" Thoroughly confused, Eve held her temples where pain now pounded and braced her elbows on her knees to support her head. "You've lost me. Stop!" she commanded when he opened his mouth to speak. "Let me think."

Massaging her temples, she went over his accusations. Since thought didn't clarify anything, she tried doing it out loud. "My uncle didn't buy my coffee maker. I did. And I bought the secondhand car because . . . because I was tired of people trying to take advantage of me simply because they knew I could afford it. I wanted to see if I'd be treated any differently if no one suspected how wealthy I am."

"Wealthy?" Adam frowned at her. "Now *I'm* confused." Then he stiffened, glaring at her once more. For a moment, he'd sounded like his old self. But the abberation had passed, and she was left with this . . . stranger. His voice was cold again as he asked, "What's the name of your company?"

Things began to add up. She'd never once mentioned the name of the business, and somehow he'd misread her explanation. "Worldwide," she said, utterly weary with apprehension. "I tried to tell you—"

"Worldwide!" The word exploded from him. "You call Worldwide a *small* electonics firm? Jeez! I'd hate to hear your definition of GE."

"GE's a conglomerate. But compared to them, Worldwide *is* small. That's what I meant."

"Well, how the hell was I supposed to know that? I thought you meant something on the order of a dog and pony show. I don't play with semantics like you do."

Her shaking had returned to play in tandem with the throb of pain in her head. She huddled under the onslaught of a migraine and asked in a small voice, "So what do we do now?"

"Do?" He laughed. "How can I trust you or anything you say? Our entire relationship has been built on deceit."

Stung, she flung up her head and winced at the familiar shooting pain. "I never lied to you."

"Well, forgive me if I don't quite believe you, Miss Sutton. It's hard to know *what* to believe when someone's hoodwinked you over a measly matter of a few million dollars! Or is it billions?" He grabbed up his suit jacket and shoved an arm into one of the sleeves.

"Millions," she muttered almost under her breath. Even if it was *hundreds* of millions. Then, stronger, "Where are you going?"

"To get roaring drunk," he tossed over his shoulder. "To try and forget I asked you to marry me tonight!"

"Wait."

She stood and struggled to remove the beautiful solitaire. She couldn't see through the film of tears obscuring her vision, but she twisted it off by feel alone. Then she heard the door slam.

Eve awoke with a start and sat up on the sofa. Then she moaned, remembering as pain speared through her head. She'd cried herself to sleep. And tears certainly hadn't helped her migraine.

Opening her swollen lids to mere slits, she stumbled into the kitchen to shut off the overhead lights. She slowly gazed at the lamp-lit room beyond. Other than a fresh stab through her eyes each time she moved them, she could see. Barely.

Turning so that she moved her whole body rather than just her eyes, she made her way to the sink and turned on the cold water tap. Wetting the dish towel, she held it to her throbbing forehead, still stunned by Adam's response to her gift and his rejection of her.

Only one clear thought surfaced after standing there in a daze for untold minutes, the same one she'd had just before falling asleep. She had to leave. A good trick since she could barely see.

Never mind; she'd manage. The only place she had to go to was the cabin. If she didn't make it that far, she at least had to get out of here.

She felt her way into the bedroom. By the time she reached the closet, she remembered to crouch rather than bend over to retrieve her suitcase. Beads of perspiration stood out on her forehead, but at least there were no disabling flashes of pain to make her black out.

Eve emptied the drawers into the case simply by upending them. Sweeping the hanging clothes into her arms, she tried to stuff them into the open bag, then couldn't close the top. She sat on the bed, removing each hanger and folding each garment, all without looking down. What she couldn't fit into the suitcase, she left.

Picking up the old-fashioned alarm clock beside the bed, she brought it close to her face and peered at the numbers. A few minutes after four. Good. No traffic; less things to run into.

She made her way through the house and pulled the door to behind her. Please, God, let the car keys be in the ignition, otherwise she'd never find them in this condition. She vaguely remembered leaving them there when she'd rushed home to shower and change so she could intercept Adam for his party.

She drove on sheer instinct until she reached the highway and could distinguish the dividing yellow marker. Then she simply followed the line. When an oncoming car nearly blinded her, she squeezed her eyes to slits. But the pain in her head grew until she was literally almost blind. The shapes ahead looked like buildings, so she pulled off and went to sleep.

When next Eve woke, it was to the long blast of a semi's airhorn; only something that large could have made such a horrendous racket. Easing her lids open, sunlight shattered her hopes for diminished pain. She fumbled in the glovebox for her sunglasses, knowing they wouldn't be much help.

Barely pausing to peer for oncoming traffic, she pulled out onto the highway. She checked her watch at the first roil of migraine-induced nausea, but couldn't read the time. She thought the dashboard clock indicated eleven. Gritting her teeth, she drove and refused to give in to her quivering stomach until she reached the cabin.

Somehow she managed to read the road signs and, within little more than a half hour, surprised herself by rolling to a stop in familiar surroundings. She knew they were familiar because when she opened the car door, Simms helped her out.

"I'm sorry, Simms. I'm afraid I'm going to be sick."

"Yes, Miss Eve, I recognize the signs. You just lean on me."

His words echoed, the last thing she remembered.

Adam first heard a hollow clumping sound before a piercing, off-key whistle nearly took off the top of his head. The thumping grew louder and vibrated through his skull.

"Well, glory be!" The voice was familiar.

Someone shook him, but he didn't want to wake up and face whoever it was. He had a feeling something terrible had happened.

"Adam, do you hear me?"

He struggled to form the words to ask the time.

"It's nine o'clock."

"Good. See ya in the mornin'."

A horrible braying laugh grated on his ears. He tried to bury his head, but his hands couldn't find anything but air.

"I've got bad news for you, boy. It *is* morning."

He could hear Sudie's words clearly now, but it took several moments for the meaning to sink through the morass of jangling nerve endings, then to connect and make sense. When it did, he sprang up . . . or at least he tried to. "What day is it?"

"Saturday."

He tried to deny it. Maybe *this* was the nightmare. "No."

"Oh, yes it is. You had a party last night, Friday, remember?"

As soon as he heard the word *party,* he remembered everything. Including the fifth of Scotch he'd tried to drink to forget. Hell, he didn't even like Scotch, but it'd been the only full bottle he could find. He managed to sit up. And wished he hadn't. But something she'd said. . . . "What time did you say it was?"

"Nine o'clock. Want I should try the clinic to see if Martha's even made it in?"

"Yeah." He breathed deeply, hoping to quell the rebellion he could feel building in his stomach. "And make some coffee. Lots of it. Please."

Sudie stopped in the doorway. "Is Eve in the same shape you're in?"

"I don't know."

He'd have given anything at that moment to relive the whole evening, excising the one moment Eve had handed him that damned envelope. He dragged himself into the shower.

He drank one cup of coffee and decided not to risk another one. As he looked around for his hat, Sudie said, "I'd better check on Eve to make sure—"

"No!" The word escaped before Adam could think. But when he saw the astonished look on his housekeeper's face, he added, "I'll stop by," and hightailed it toward the door.

But she had the last word. "I don't know why you're in such an all-fired hurry. Unless things have changed, everyone in town will have heard about the party. No one's going to expect you to be all bright eyed and bushy tailed today."

Great, just bloody great, he thought as he gunned the truck. Now he had to see Eve in the shape he was in because Sudie would be watching to make sure he did. He could barely think, let alone try to make sense of the shambles of his life.

He pulled into the driveway, trying to remember how things had been left last night. All he could remember clearly was his anger over what Eve had done. Knowing his temper where Emery was concerned, he'd probably said a lot of things he shouldn't have. Well, he couldn't sit out here all day. He'd better face the music.

He climbed down, cursing the blinding sunshine as he made his way to the house. When he opened the screen door, he noticed the interior door stood open a few inches. He knocked, wincing at the noise. "Eve?"

When he received no answer, he pushed the door open and called her name again. He stood undecided a moment, then stepped inside. All he had to do, he reminded himself as he made his way back to the bedroom, was explain why he was there and mention something about getting together tonight to talk things out. Hopefully by then he'd be up to it.

The first thing Adam saw as he stepped through the doorway were dresser drawers on the bed, then the open, bare closet. Unbelieving, he found himself standing by the bed and gazing into empty drawers and at a pile of folded clothes.

Where had she gone? And why?

She'd left some clothes; that meant she had to return at some point. Without realizing it, he'd already moved into the hall toward Eve's studio. The tension in his shoulders relaxed at its normal appearance: a partially completed canvas rested on an easel and tubes of paint lay scattered on an adjacent tray. Several completed canvases lined one wall. Here too was evidence that she'd be back.

Thinking he might have missed a note in the kitchen, he returned there but found nothing to indicate why Eve had left or where she'd gone. A few steps took him to the back of a sofa. The long legal sheets of the deed lay scattered on the coffee table and floor. As he picked up the last page, a sparkle caught his eye. A sunbeam ignited the solitaire's fire as he picked up the engagement ring he'd given Eve.

He didn't want to think of why she'd taken it off. There'd been hope he'd be able to straighten everything out with her when he could think again. Her disappearance and the ring made him wonder. Where the hell had she gone? And why hadn't she left some sort of message? With his anger stoked anew, he hurried away, taking both the ring and the deed.

Fourteen

By early afternoon, Adam had tired of saying he didn't know where Eve was and looked forward to being able to bury himself in work at the farm. At least there he wouldn't keep running into someone wanting to know Eve's whereabouts.

When his office door opened, he didn't even look up. "Let's close up, Martha. Thank heavens it's been a light day. If your head feels—"

"There's nothing wrong with *my* head, thank you." Adam snapped to attention at the sound of Jane's voice. "Though Eve was kind enough to invite me to your birthday party."

He almost groaned at having to deal with her now, then noticed

she looked friendly for a change. He climbed to his feet and tried
to be cordial. "Jane, what can I do for you?"

"Well, I think we might be able to help each other." For the
first time in his life, he saw Jane looking uncertain as her gaze
flickered away from his. "I plan to open a riding stable, on a
piece of Arnmunson's property, and I . . . I wondered if I could
count on you to be my vet." Her gaze returned to his almost
defiantly with her request.

Adam shook his head, sure he'd misunderstood. "I'm sorry,
I'm having trouble concentrating today. Did you say Arn's land?"

"It's really mine now, since I convinced him to sell me a few
acres for the stables. I'm still dickering about details on riding
trails."

"But why go to all that trouble when your dad—"

"This had nothing to do with my father." A flush rose under
her tan. "Eve made me see that I could do this on my own since
he wouldn't let me get involved with *his* horses."

"Eve!"

For the first time, Jane smiled. "She really is something, isn't
she? But she was right, too. I feel I'm accomplishing something
and, since I love horses, the riding stable is a natural." She looked
diffident for a moment, then said, "So how about it? Will you let
bygones be bygones and be my vet?"

Bemused, Adam nodded. "And congratulations," he said, shaking her hand. "I think it's a terrific idea."

He walked Jane out, wondering at her transformation and how
Eve had brought it about. Her last comment left him more confused than ever.

"I'm glad I was able to handle this on my own, but it was
sweet of Eve to tell me about the Eden Foundation. Tell her I
won't forget it."

She waved and ran off before he could ask what she meant.
Adam stood staring after her in the hot sun, one thought upper-
most in his mind: Eve had been right about Jane. He'd been pigheaded—and wrong. It seemed he didn't know everything, and
doubt assailed him.

Doubts and questions multiplied when his friend Fisk pulled
up alongside him at a stop sign a block from the clinic. "Hey,
Adam," he shouted through their lowered windows, "tell Eve I

heard from the Eden Foundation this morning. I got the loan."
Wearing a smile that wouldn't quit, his friend waved farewell
when a car behind them honked.

The Eden Foundation again. What the hell?

Adam took his questions home to Sudie, hoping she'd be able
to tell him what was going on.

She stood staring at him, her hands planted on her plump hips.
"You mean Eve never told you anything about the foundation and
what we've been doing?"

"No, but she worked on something in the office. I think she
mentioned a marketing plan, but what has that got to do with this
mysterious Eden Foundation?"

"Hmmph. And here I thought the two of you were closer than
aphids on roses."

"Sudie," he warned, in no mood to be teased or hassled.

"Oh, all right, don't get your dander up. But why don't you
ask her yourself?"

"If I knew where she was, I would." Knowing he had no choice,
Adam explained about the signs of Eve's departure. "I'd hoped
she would have called one of us by now and explained."

Sudie shook her head. Frowning, she said, "I wish I'd known
about this earlier. It doesn't make any sense."

"Nothing makes sense today, but what are you talking about?"

"About a half hour after you left this morning, Eve's chauffeur
stopped by, wanting to know if I knew where to find her."

"Her chauffeur!"

"Yeah," she said with a grin. "That's how he introduced himself.
I sent him into town to Alice's. Thought that's where she'd be."

He sat down and rubbed his throbbing head. "People have been
calling me all day looking for Eve. How does she fit into the
Eden Foundation?"

Sudie explained how Eve's uncle had put them in touch with
the organization and what they'd been able to accomplish. "Eve
was a big help, telling people how to improve their business plans,
but that isn't all she did.

"She found an outlet for Granny Thompson to sell her quilts.
With twenty of the things tucked away, her granddaughter Gloria
won't have to worry about money for college. Not with the schol-
arship Eve steered her toward.

"And Alice too," Sudie added with no lessening of enthusiasm. "There was so much interest stirred up over art from all those new residents that Eve convinced Alice they could hold classes. They even found a sculptor. Alice is thrilled at the possibilities. It's given *me* a new lease on life," she said with a huge grin.

Adam silently added the names of Jane and Fisk to the list of those Eve had helped. He groaned and lowered his head to the table.

Eve could have called her chauffeur to wisk her away when she'd had car trouble. But she hadn't. Not only had she stayed among them, but her actions showed she loved being part of the community. Was it possible she had seen him as simply another person who needed help achieving a dream?

He groaned again, remembering the night of his birthday. She'd given him something beyond price, and he'd thrown her gift of love—not to mention the deed—back in her face.

Sheba moved beside his chair and whined. Adam absently petted her, saying, "Oh, Lord. What have I done?"

Eve awoke. Even through the dim light, she recognized her bedroom in Lake Forest. She sighed and closed her eyes. But after a moment, her eyelids fluttered open again. Something didn't feel right.

"Well, child, you waking up at last?"

Tilly's voice came from beyond her line of vision. She reached for her hand and held it next to her cheek. "Tilly. I'm so glad to be home."

"You feeling better now, sugar?"

"I think so." She shifted her gaze to where Tilly sat on the side of the bed; no pain accompanied the movement. "What happened, did I have another one of my migraines?"

"Yes. Do you remember anything about it?"

After thinking a moment, Eve raised her left hand and stared at it. No ring. "Unfortunately, yes. I was driving to the cabin, but I don't recall getting there." She looked back at Tilly. "For some reason though, I seem to remember seeing Simms."

Tilly chuckled. "You just about gave him a heart attack, fainting dead away on him yesterday."

"Yesterday!" Eve squeezed Tilly's hand. "What day is it?"

Her maid smoothed back the hair from Eve's face. "Now, you're not to get yourself all worked up. I'll answer your questions, but you have to stay calm." When Eve relaxed her grip, she said, "This is Sunday. I had a real nice conversation last night with a lady by the name of Sudie. Your uncle thought I should call and explain how you'd had to return home because he needed you."

"Is Uncle Robb here?"

"Not now, but he'll be back here later today. I can't keep that man away."

Eve smiled at the false complaining note in her voice; Tilly was almost as fond of Uncle Robb as she was. The solidity of their unquestioned love bolstered her battered feelings and gave her something to hang onto.

She reminded herself of that again Sunday evening when Simms handed her the sketch pad he'd taken from her car along with her suitcase. He grinned and told her he liked her bumper stickers. Momentarily distracted, she realized she'd become so used to the silly things that she'd forgotten to remove them.

Flipping through the pages of her sketch pad later, she showed Tilly the drawings and explained who everyone was. Until she came to the last one. She'd forgotten she'd drawn Adam from memory, his Stetson tipped forward and that damned sexy grin showing beneath his mustache.

"My, my, my!" Tilly said, admiring the sketch. "Who's that?"

When Eve explained about her rescuer, Tilly said, "I wasn't too sure about that valley and all those people you mentioned. But with him around, sugar, it might be worth being sentenced to a life of public transportation."

"I've got news for you, Tilly. They don't even *have* public transportation."

Not that it mattered. She wouldn't have minded anything as long as she had Adam's love. With him beside her, she could even deal with the office on a daily basis. Thanks to her uncle though, she wouldn't have to much longer.

If Eve had needed any clarification about her preference of lifestyles, the matter was settled for her the next two days as she wound up business matters and avoided Richard. She'd even begun to wonder if she'd been wrong in running away. She had helped Jane to help herself. Why didn't the same lesson apply to herself?

Adam was worth fighting for. She just had to think if there was a way to make him realize how stubborn he was being about Hartwig. She worried over the problem during the board meeting where her uncle's preparations helped ensure a majority vote for an employee buy out.

Eve avoided looking directly at Richard throughout the meeting and escaped to her office to clean out her desk. She was almost free. She picked up an empty box and began to fill it while trying to figure out what to say to Adam.

When her office door opened ten minutes later, she was leaning over her bottom drawer. "I think this is everything, Jean. When you've finished packing my books, just give Simms a call to pick up the boxes."

She closed her drawer and noticed the shiny, squared-off brown leather boot tips standing beside her desk. She raised her head slowly, hardly daring to hope. He wore his Stetson tilted at a familiar angle, the one that teased with a glimpse of his hazel eyes and the same sexy grin that always made her pulse jump.

His name escaped on a little sigh. "Adam."

"Hello, beautiful."

Then she was in his arms, being squeezed until she had no breath left. She struggled to inhale and push him away so she could see his face. "What are you doing here?"

Adam loosened his embrace and feasted on the sight of Eve's smiling face. At least she was happy to see him; he'd been afraid she would refuse to talk to him. And he would have deserved it.

"I came to apologize and throw myself on your mercy. If you can find it in your heart to forgive whatever terrible things I must have said to you, I want to take you home."

"Oh, Adam. I'd decided this morning that I made a mistake in leaving like I did. I was going to confront you and—"

He didn't give her a chance to say any more. They were headed in the same direction and that was all that mattered. He lowered his head and covered her lips with a hunger deeper than he'd known existed.

He scattered kisses across her brow, her temple and along her jaw, saying, "I feel like such an idiot for having doubted your motives. Can you ever forgive me? I'm a pigheaded fool who doesn't deserve his luck."

Eve stopped his rambling apology with her lips, relief and joy mingling to make her lightheaded with happiness. She threaded her fingers through the soft fall of Adam's hair over his collar and held on when he lifted his head. There remained only one hurdle.

"Adam," she said, trying to get his attention when his lips continued to trail down her neck. She pushed at his shoulder until he looked at her. "There's just one thing. I have to make you see that by reacting as you do to Hartwig, you're letting him win. It's like you haven't progressed beyond where you were emotionally when he pulled his first dirty trick."

"I always said you were smart, City Girl." He kissed the tip of her nose, wanting to do so much more, but knowing he had to reassure Eve on this important point.

"That's pretty much the conclusion I came to on Sunday when I finally got my head working again. I realized I have a knee-jerk reaction to anything that has to do with Emery. It clouds my judgment and almost cost me the most precious thing I've ever known."

His kiss this time remained gentle as he tried to set her mind at ease. He withdrew only far enough to speak. "I have to get beyond that mind set in order to deal rationally with Emery. I know I can do it. Will you take a chance on me?"

Her eyes sparkled as she said, "Does that mean I get my ring back?"

He let go of her long enough to fish in his pocket. "I just happened to bring it along in case I got lucky . . . for the second time." He put the ring on her finger, saying, "This time it stays there. Forever."

His kiss came hard and insistent, and Eve gave herself up to the glorious rush of sensation that only Adam could cause.

When his hands molded her body to his and his breath became more ragged, he whispered, "I think we'd better get out of here before we shock your secretary."

She pulled out of his arms with a smile. "I agree. Come on, let's hurry."

Jean looked slightly apprehensive when Eve opened her office door. Then she saw Uncle Robb beaming at her from the doorway.

"Something tells me this was a conspiracy," she said, going into his arms.

"I had to do something to convince him to wait until today," her uncle said. "He was all set to kidnap you yesterday until I explained the importance of this morning's board meeting." He shook Adam's hand. "I take it you don't plan a long engagement."

"No, sir, just as soon as we can arrange things."

As they left her office, Eve found they had to run the gauntlet of good wishes from others who'd heard rumors and gathered along the hall. She'd made friends at Worldwide without knowing it.

They finally made it to the elevator, and she punched the call button before a cold voice hailed her sharply. "Eve!"

She turned to face Richard, dreading a scene. He looked at Adam with a sneer that grew as his gaze traveled the long length of Adam's body to his boots. "Well, at least I know now what you found in Wisconsin to occupy so much of your time. I must say I'm surprised. I thought you more discriminating."

Adam's brows lowered, and she tried to diffuse the situation. "Richard, you gave up the privilege of being able to say anything about my behavior by your own. Our engagement was over a long time before I returned your ring." She pulled at Adam, trying to get him into the elevator. "Let's go."

He removed her hand from his arm. "Just a minute." He turned back to Richard and regarded him coolly. "I have something for you," he said, taking a step forward.

Without warning, Adam's arm shot out and his fist connected with the underside of Richard's jaw. Dead silence reigned from those in the area as Richard flew backward and landed on the carpet in a sprawl.

After a moment he raised a shaky hand to his face, and Adam rubbed his knuckles as he stood over him. "I promised myself I'd do that if I ever got the chance. You're lucky I'm a gentleman. Otherwise I'd wipe the floor with you."

Settling his Stetson, he turned to Eve. Before she knew what he intended, he scooped her up in his arms. With the grin she loved so well, he said, "I'm taking you back to our valley where you belong."

Epilogue

Eve set out their picnic lunch in her favorite spot. She never tired of this view from the meadow where she could look down the entire length of their valley, now called Eden Farms. She'd seen it in every season over the last two years and had decided Adam was right. It did recharge your batteries.

High-pitched babble floated to her on the warm breeze, and she hurried to find the bibs as Adam appeared through the trees with their fifteen-month-old twins in each arm.

She looked at her husband in amusement and rose to relieve him of half his burden. "Were you successful in introducing your offspring to their ancestors?"

He settled on the blanket and reached for a bib. "Well, my granddad thought you were never too young to learn. My earliest memory was of him showing me the headstones in the family plot. Of course," he said with a grin, "he only had one to keep track of while I've got two."

Eve handed her children some finger food. "I hope you still think all this was worth it," she said, pushing a puppy away from Ramsey's lunch, "when we've hauled everyone back down to the wagon again."

She tossed the tiny replica of Sheba a biscuit of his own. The smell of food had brought the three other puppies at a run, and she gave them biscuits, too, to keep them off the blanket. Sheba looked liked she was counting noses and finally settled next to Eve.

Eve looked up in time to see Adam remove the food from her daughter's hand that Regina had decided to share with one of the puppies. He laughed as he tossed it a short distance and watched the puppies scramble for it. "I begin to see what you mean. We're going to spend the whole time playing watchdog. Excuse the language, Sheba," he added, leaning over to give her a dog biscuit of her own.

Placating his daughter with some more food, he tossed tidbits to the puppies to keep them away from the children. "I'll definitely think the trip was worth it," Adam said, settling back down on the blanket, "because I have a surprise for you." He looked at his watch. "In exactly one-half hour, we'll pack up the twin's supplies, put the puppies in the carriers, and tote the whole tribe back down to the wagon where we will be met."

Anticipation brightened the smile she gave him. "And then what?"

"And then," he said with the sexy grin that never failed to warm her, "then we return posthaste ourselves to revive old memories."

"Ummm. One of my favorite pastimes."

She gave him a lingering kiss and packed away their own food to protect it from the dogs. Lunch over, they washed the twins, changed their diapers, and packed everything up. With her child already yawning in her backpack, Eve mounted Treasure with Adam's help. Then, loaded with the other twin, he mounted Lucky for the trip down the hill.

As soon as they started walking the horses, the child in Adam's backpack started babbling. He cast her a startled look. "I thought *you* had Gina."

Well acquainted with her daughter's desire to talk while riding, she said, "Nope, I pulled a fast one. I thought I'd let you have her while I used the quiet time to plan my husband's seduction."

His shout of laughter woke Ramsey, who fussed for a minute before settling back down. These Sunday excursions were one of Eve's favorite times. She loved roaming the valley with Adam and the children, but she also looked forward to turning the twins over for a few hours to Tilly and Simms or Sudie and Carl, whoever won the toss for the day. If Uncle Robb was around, the two couples had to fight for their chance at the children. This was the first time they'd brought the twins to the meadow, and she watched with interest to see who would meet them.

Eve had tried to retire Tilly and Simms, but had been only partially successful. Since they wanted to move with her, they'd

lived in Adam's grandfather's house until a suite of their own had
been added to the big house, as it was now called. She expanded
it again with a suite for her uncle and a huge family room that
tumbled down the side of the hill in back with a spectacular reverse view of the valley. Tilly ruled the nursery with help who
went home at night, and Simms continued to run errands and
drive anyone who would let him.

When she saw the three people waiting for them by the wagon,
Eve hid her smile. Tilly and Simms never failed to amaze her. If
something involved the children, they did whatever was necessary
to become a part of it.

"You've been taking riding lessons behind my back," she said
to them, reining in Treasure.

Her uncle came over to help her dismount without disturbing
the sleeping baby. From the cushioned bed of the wagon where
she waited with two traveling cribs, Tilly smiled smugly. "Like
Sudie's always telling me, 'Who says an old dog can't learn new
tricks?' "

With her puppies offloaded in their carriers to the wagon, Sheba
jumped up to supervise their return home. Adam and Eve waved
to them as Simms started the team and the wagon slowly rolled
off, the three saddlehorses trailing behind. Then Adam looked
over at her with a grin. "Want to race back?"

It wasn't even a contest; he always beat her. He pulled a chilled
bottle of wine from the spring while Eve unpacked their lunch
once more. She laughed when she saw the cantaloupe, which reminded her of her first excursion up here.

She pushed a piece of it into Adam's mouth, saying, "I'm glad
Sheba's not with us today."

"If I'd had to tie her to the wagon, I was determined she
wouldn't return with us."

"Take your seductions seriously, do you?"

"Yes, especially when it's hard to get my wife off alone during
the day, all to myself."

"Well," Eve said, leaning over and unbuttoning his shirt, "do
you remember the last time?"

"Hmmm, let me see." His grin turned wicked as he pulled her
down beside him and started to work on the buttons of the silk

blouse she'd worn to tempt him. "I think the last time was about a month ago. We christened your new studio.

"By the way," he added, trailing his lips down the opening his fingers made, "turning my granddad's house into a studio and gallery was a stroke of genius. Now we'll have someplace warm to escape to besides the barn during the winter."

"All the better to seduce you, my dear," Eve said in a throaty voice. "Although I have fond memories of the hayloft."

"So do I, but I've learned to enjoy comfort."

"Speaking of comfort, would you mind terribly having the workmen back again?"

"No, but why?"

Eve squirmed as his lips moved back up her midriff. "I figure if we get them started right away, we might just make it in time."

Adam raised his head. "Make what in time?"

"The new addition we need on the house." When he stared at her blankly, she pulled him toward her so she could watch his expression. "Before the next snow flies, we need to expand the nursery again."

His gaze dropped to her breasts, already tender and beginning to swell in preparation for their next child. His stunned expression turned to joy, and he kissed her thoroughly. When he raised his head, he said, "Is there anything I can get you? Is there anything you want?"

"Yes," Eve replied, pulling his mouth back down to hers. "My conjugal rights."